THE SINGLE LIFE

THE SINGLE LIFE

•

Kate McKeever

AVALON BOOKS
NEW YORK

Published by Thomas Bouregy & Co., Inc.
160 Madison Avenue, New York, NY 10016

Library of Congress Cataloging-in-Publication Data

McKeever, Kate, 1957–
    The single life / Kate McKeever.
        p.   cm.
    ISBN 0-8034-9752-0 (acid-free paper)
    1. Journalists—Fiction.   2. Atlanta (Ga.)—Fiction.   I. Title.
    PS3613.C5526S56   2006
    813'.6—dc22

                                        2005028540

PRINTED IN THE UNITED STATES OF AMERICA
ON ACID-FREE PAPER
BY HADDON CRAFTSMEN, BLOOMSBURG, PENNSYLVANIA

For Mom and Dad, who taught me to plant my feet
firmly and reach for the stars.

Thanks to the SMRW girls, who keep me going when I want to give up and my critique group (Katie, Juli, and Kerrie). You've read it and reread it. My thanks to Donna W. who never let me quit, and reminds me to work. And thanks to my family, Nancy, Ken, and Terry, along with the in-laws and nieces/nephews. You may not understand me but thanks for the love and support. And thanks to the faith that sustains me.

Chapter One

"**I** won't do it. I won't be a guinea pig just to satisfy Wheaton's need for a ratings boost." Delaney Morgan slammed the ladies' room door closed and stalked to the bank of washbasins flanking the wall. She glared into the mirror as her friend's reflection calmly eyed her. "I mean it, I *won't* do it."

"Then you'll never get reassigned out of obits." Caroline Paul extracted a pack of cigarettes from her skintight khaki skirt pocket and pulled a slightly creased cigarette from the pack.

Laney automatically opened the old-fashioned crank window at the far wall. She ran a hand through her short brown hair. "As if he'll give me another job. I've been there longer than anyone has."

"Stop writing cute little vignettes about the dearly

departed and you might get another desk." Caro reached into the edge of the soap dispenser and came out with a crumpled book of matches. She grimaced as she held the lit match to her cigarette. "God, I feel like I'm back in high school, sneaking a smoke in the john."

"Quit," Laney shot back unsympathetically.

"Yeah right, and gain twenty pounds. I work hard to keep this figure." Caro took a long draw. "No kidding. You have to take the assignment. If you don't Wheaton will pick another single female writer and you'll be stuck in the morgue forever."

Laney opened a stall door and dropped the toilet lid down. She sank onto it and propped her chin on her hand. "I know. But to get assigned *this*. It's embarrassing. 'The Single Life' column. It's like a spoof on a rerun of a bad TV show."

"Look on the bright side. The newspaper will pay you for going out on dates. Dinners, sporting events—"

"Going out with men I don't know, may not want to know. And picture this. I'll be seen as the only woman in Atlanta who can't get a date unless her boss sets it up."

"You're being silly. No one will think that, and you know it." Caro puffed on her cigarette.

Laney sprang from her seat and eyed her reflection in the mirror. "I'm not that bad looking, am I? I have all my teeth, no visible laugh lines, and not too many extra lumps and curves." She turned sideways to peer at her backside. "And nothing's going south too fast."

"You're cute," her friend muttered around her fast shrinking cigarette. "With your hair cut like that, you're really cute."

"Great. Just what a twenty-eight-year-old wants to hear. Cute," Laney muttered, scowling at her image. But Caroline was right. She favored a young Sally Field more than Ashley Judd, and would always look like the best friend or the girl next door.

"Well, some guys think cute is . . . cute." Caro shrugged an elegant shoulder and stubbed out her cigarette. She lifted the toilet cover Laney had perched on and dropped the butt into the bowl then flushed. As she washed her hands she eyed Laney through the mirror. "Any guy who got you would be lucky."

"Yeah." In her experience, the only luck guys found in her friendship was that she could introduce them to beautiful women like Caroline.

"Look at it this way, Laney. If you agree to this assignment, you'll finally get the byline you've been working for."

The two exited the bathroom and headed to their separate sections—Caroline to her society column, and Laney to the tiny space she called her office.

Caro might have a point, Laney mused. After all, the whole purpose of working for a newspaper was to get bigger and better assignments, to bring the breaking news to the public. What with the Internet and cable news programs, though, print journalism had to fill in different gaps. Maybe a column on single life in the metro area could work. If she could bring herself to go out on dates, on assignment.

She slowed as she approached the cubicle she used as her work space. Grant Stone stood just inside the enclosure, taking up too much room. If he weren't so darned arrogant, she thought, he'd be attractive. Over six-feet tall, with a strong, muscled body, the senior newspaper man took up a lot of room just standing there. Add to the equation his dark brown hair, intense brown eyes, and rumbling voice, and he had women looking him over and judging him gorgeous.

She stopped outside her assigned work area; there just wasn't room in the six-by-six-foot area for another person. Her temper, somewhat calmed by her talk with Caroline, simmered. Stone looked as if he was bored out of his mind. What was he doing there, anyway? Her days of fetch and carry for him as an intern were long gone.

He fiddled with her computer animals, messing up the arrangement of the collection.

"Can I help you?"

He glanced away from the small figurine of a cartoon cat she displayed, among other toys, on her computer. "You Morgan?"

"Yes," she snipped. He knew darn well who she was. After all, she'd spent over a year as one of the legion of gophers he ordered around before the obits assignment came through.

"We need to talk." He sat on the edge of the desk and eyed her. Laney waited, curious but silent.

"About what?"

"Your new assignment."

Laney groaned silently. Did everyone in the office know about this? And why was Grant Stone, reporter extraordinaire, interested?

"Are you coming in here?" He gestured toward her desk.

The air thinned in her area, as if he were taking his and part of her share of oxygen, and Laney glared at him then edged around to her chair. Sitting there gave her a much needed feeling of comfort, amongst her papers, notes and funeral home flyers.

"What do you want to know about my assignment?" She wasn't adding any more wood to the gossip fire in this place. Even if Grant didn't engage in the water cooler gossip, he'd surely have heard about the peon reporter who couldn't get a date.

"The Single Life column. Wheaton said he'd given you the assignment. Are you going to do it?"

"Of course I am, why shouldn't I?" *Where did that come from? Yes, I volunteered to gargle ground glass in a public forum, thanks.*

"What the hell possessed you to do that?" he barked, and Laney frowned at him.

"Whose business is it if I did agree to the column? It's no trouble to you." She leaned back in her chair, careful not to overtax the sprung swivel feature.

He stood and began pacing the two or three steps it took to cover the distance of her cubicle. "It sure as hell does matter to me. I have to oversee the thing."

Laney's chair sprang upright. "What?"

"You didn't know?" His eyes narrowed as he studied her. "The column will be written by both of us."

"Uh uh. Mr. Wheaton promised me a byline if I agreed to the column. Nobody's going to horn in on that." *A byline in a successful column might get me out of this morgue.*

"I didn't 'horn in.' I was sucked into the thing by Wheaton."

"How?"

"Never mind how." He halted his pacing and glared at her.

Laney opened her mouth, ready to defend her side, to deny wanting the column then reconsidered. Maybe it wasn't the best assignment in the world, but it belonged to *her*.

"Look, I don't want to know your business, but the column, the byline, is *mine*."

"Oh, you'll get the byline," Grant replied. "Or rather half of it. According to Wheaton, The Single Life is going to be from the male and female view."

"So, you'll have to do the dating thing too?" She tried to dampen the hope in her voice. If Grant also became a lab rat, she wouldn't appear too desperate. But why hadn't the editor explained this to her, himself?

"No way. I get to be your shadow." He grimaced. "I have to follow you and be an independent observer."

"Jeez."

"Yeah, I get to be your chaperone." His tone sounded as horrified as she was. He slumped back down on the only other seating in her cubicle, the edge of her desk.

Laney tried to absorb his words. She was putting her ego, her career, and even her reputation on the line for half a byline? To write a singles column would probably seal her fate as a fluff reporter, not a hard-hitting journalist.

"What a mess," she muttered.

"Right, and you're responsible."

"Me? Tell me again how I'm to blame for something I've been assigned." *Is this guy determined to make me dislike him?*

"You could've said no. Could have held out for a different story." He leaned forward to drive home his point.

"And gotten fired. Do you realize how long I've been writing obits?" She faced him down.

"So, you'd find another job, keep pitching ideas to the desk." He was so close she could make out flecks of green in the brown eyes glaring at her.

"Yeah, like there's a ton of jobs out there for obit writers." *God, my life is depressing.*

"So, you have to sacrifice both our careers. No thanks, I'll handle Wheaton myself."

"And do what? Take the byline completely?" She wouldn't put it past him.

"No. And get out of writing a column with a novice that doesn't know when to throw in the towel." He stood and stalked out of her cubicle.

Laney counted to ten, twenty, and stopped at four hundred and thirty-nine before she was able to return to her computer. *Let him get out of the column,* she thought. She would have the byline and no arrogant busybody watching over her shoulder.

By the end of the workday, Laney was determined. She'd take the assignment and make the most of it. Whether Grant Stone liked having her as a partner or not. The fact he didn't want her to take the assignment played no part in it. Right, and she would win the Pulitzer for the column this year. In the meantime, maybe it'd be a good idea to look for another job. Just in case.

Grant tugged at his loosened tie as he walked toward his car. The parking lot of *The Globe* was clearing out, many of the employees already gone for the day. He'd stayed trying to convince Wheaton to let him travel to the Middle East on a story. With no success.

"You're a mainstay in Atlanta, Stone. Everyone loves your stuff."

Yeah, right. And the fact he'd been Wheaton's only real competition for editor didn't influence the rush to assign him baby-sitting duties. You'd think four years would have reduced the animosity the older man felt toward Grant, but he made a practice of passing over Grant for younger and less experienced writers. Prime stories too.

At this rate, I'll be on the obits beat with little Morgan in a year. Unbidden, her face, framed with short brown curls, sprang to mind. She looked like a sprite or some godforsaken elf, he mused. Not what a newspaper reporter should look like at all. But cute.

He unlocked his car and opened the door. As he waited for the worst of the summer heat to escape the auto after baking all day, Grant's eye caught a movement to his left.

Delaney Morgan strode to her ancient Volkswagen bug with a bouncy, athletic stride. She either didn't see him or ignored his presence, and quickly entered her compact and drove away.

Grant swore and sat on the blazing hot leather seat of his low-slung Corvette. He unfastened a couple more buttons on his shirt, seeking some respite from the heat that the beleaguered air conditioner couldn't touch.

Delaney didn't deserve his ire; she didn't have any role in his battle with Wheaton. Yet, it appeared she would be a prime player, since he'd have to watch over her for several months. And there was no way he could get out of the column and stay with the paper.

"Maybe it's time to leave," he grumbled, and drove to the lot exit. It was past time to look for another job. He'd start checking online when he got home.

Laney spent the evening online, trying to find a job she could apply for. Nothing. No openings for creative obit writers with a penchant for poetry. She woke the next morning with a headache from her dreams of meeting men who took her home to meet Mother Bates and Lizzie Borden.

She pulled into the last vacant space at the paper, the one behind the dumpster, and held her breath against the stench as she exited the car.

Grant's racy sports car resided proudly in his spot, next to the managing editor. She eyed the vehicle; it figured Stone had a plaything like that. Low, masculine, and powerful. Like Grant.

"And both with gas to spare." She resisted the urge to kick the tires as she passed the gleaming Corvette. He'd always raised a strong reaction from her, from the secret crush she'd had on him as an intern to the current dread at the prospect of working in close proximity to him, of being overshadowed by him. But he was a great reporter, going after a story when the leads didn't appear to be present.

Caro joined her at the entrance to the vintage brick building for their morning stop at the small coffee shop next door. As they waited for their coffee orders, Laney filled in her friend on the previous afternoon's news.

"How'd Grant get roped into the job? Wasn't he a favorite of the managing editor? I heard he was even considered for the city editor position." Caroline cautiously sipped her grande skim latte.

"Extra whipped cream," Laney directed the attendant making her iced cappuccino, then turned to Caroline. "I don't know what he did but Stone must have ticked somebody off, 'cause the only way he'd get an assignment like this would be for flirting with an editor's wife or something."

She glanced at Caroline for the friendly affirmation she always got. Instead, her pal was staring behind her, eyes and mouth wide.

Laney shut her eyes and groaned. Only one person could be behind that expression. *Maybe if I ignore—*

"Who should I befriend to get out of this job? Any volunteers or suggestions?" The dry voice murmured in her ear, too close. She could smell his cologne and feel the heat from his body. Way too close.

"Well, Morgan?"

Laney shot Caroline a glare. Why hadn't she alerted her that the enemy was within hearing distance?

She huffed a breath and turned to greet dark eyes shining with laughter. "I was speaking metaphorically."

He grinned and leaned against a display of travel mugs, one hand in his dark tan pants pocket. "No, no. Tell me who I can buddy up to to get out of a baby-sitting job and I'll get right on it." He gestured with his free hand, emphasizing a chest entirely too broad to be that of a newspaperman.

"Maybe Mr. Phipps?" she croaked.

"*Mr.* Phipps, the managing editor? Not his wife? Daughter? Hmm?" He looked as if he was considering the possibility. "Naw. Guess I'll have to gather supplies for Smores and rent some DVDs for the slumber party." He stepped around her to place his order, then turned again, this time with a Styrofoam cup in his hand.

"Here's your coffee. Extra whipped cream. See you at the office, *partner*."

When Laney took her coffee she brushed fingertips with him, barely avoiding a flinch at the flash of heat the touch engendered. She sipped at the hot brew and glowered. It wasn't fair, he could infuriate her and be so attractive at the same time.

So he thought of the column as a baby-sitting job, huh? Well, she'd show him. She nudged Caro then led the way out of the coffee shop toward the office building.

"What are you planning?" Caro grinned knowingly.

"Not sure, but something. Definitely something."

When she arrived at her desk Laney had a message to report to the city editor's office that afternoon. She spent the morning working on her obits column, all the while concocting excuses and arguments for doing the column alone.

At three o'clock sharp she entered Mr. Wheaton's office and seated herself in a chair beside Stone. Other than a brief glance she avoided eye contact with him, though she figured it was a little immature. Give her time to get used to having him as a partner, and she'd be able to glare him down with the best of them.

She eyed the editor, seated at a pathologically neat desk. His job, overseeing the city beat, from society to crime, gave Wheaton a huge amount of power and he obviously reveled in it. His facial expressions ranged from superior to condescending, depending on the audience. Now, he began to outline the column timeline then stopped midway through a sentence.

"What's up with the two of you? Already offended her sensibilities, Grant?"

"Not at all. Just a difference of opinion," Grant drawled.

"About what?" He might think he was her boss but she wouldn't let Wheaton get away with treating her like a cub reporter. Though, technically she was.

"About our roles in the column," Laney inserted. "Sir, both Grant and I believe I can handle the column on my own."

Grant eyed her with what she hoped was a gleam of respect in his eyes. Yeah, she could stand up for herself. Well, heck, it was both of their wishes that he didn't get that assignment. He actually smiled at her, and was that a wink? Couldn't be. He didn't like her, did he?

"Yeah, Delaney and I have spoken about the column. She's perfectly capable of doing it solo."

Wheaton shook his head and smirked at Grant. "The column is in both names. The whole idea is to get both the male and female viewpoint of the whole singles dating thing." He leaned forward to emphasize his point. "If you do this right, you'll be the hottest newspaper duo since Lois and Clark." His tone implied he wished the opposite.

"Or Lucy and Desi." Her voice was low but the choked off chuckle from Grant indicated he heard.

He glanced at her again, his eyes trailing her shape. Suddenly, her sleeveless summer dress held all the cover of a bikini. The dress' hemline, just above her knees, didn't provide near enough material to cover her from the warmth of his gaze. Out of the blue, a man who barely noticed her in the newsroom seemed to be interested. Too bad the attraction was her body, rather than her writing ability.

Wheaton's voice called her back to reality, and Laney quietly blew a breath over the moist upper lip she'd developed.

"So, get over whatever misgivings you have and let's decide on a plan of action. Mr. Phipps is expecting good things out of this column." Wheaton scribbled something on his date book.

"Mr. Phipps? The column is his idea?" Grant straightened in his chair, his gaze suddenly sharp.

Wheaton preened. "No, it was mine. But he liked it and we have a good chance of making something out of it."

And if the column succeeded, Wheaton would take all the credit, Laney steamed.

"I've done some research into the singles' scene—" she began.

"Bet you have," drawled Grant, his voice silky smooth.

She frowned at him. "There are several avenues we

can take. I can interview people involved in speed dating, matchmaking services, and—"

"No. I already told you, I want first-person accounts. I want *you* to do the speed dating—what is that, anyway? Never mind, you'll get matched by a matchmaking service, go online with your personal profile. Add a bar scene article and we can get a good run from this."

The queasy feeling in her stomach increased until Laney briefly considered running to the bathroom. No, she took a deep breath. Grant would see that as a weakness.

"How long?" He didn't sound too comfy either.

"Who knows? Six months, maybe. With all the permutations of personal ads, getting set up and so on, we can make this puppy pay off. We'll review it after a few weeks to see how it's going." Wheaton looked entirely too proud of himself.

"But if I have to go out on the dates, what's he going to be doing? Chaperone?" Laney tilted her head toward Grant, refusing to meet his mocking gaze. Lord, he was right. He *was* going to be baby-sitting her.

"No, Grant'll be doing some interviews with participants and organizers of the events, as well as getting an outsider's view of the whole setup. Then both of you will do an article on the impact, if any, the event had on you, your impressions and so on. I haven't decided if we're going to run the articles together in a face-off format, or one opinion in the paper one day and the other following it . . ."

As they left the office, Laney and Grant eyed each other.

"You know, much as I hate to admit it, Wheaton could have something. If we do this right, the column could be a showstopper." He ran his hand across his forehead as he spoke.

"I think I hear a but coming. What?" Laney folded her arms across her chest and waited.

"You have to date with an audience and I have to help you pick 'em out."

Yippee. Now that sounds like fun.

Chapter Two

"'Find your special someone with our free personal ads.' Jeez, how hokey can you get? *The Globe* wouldn't be caught dead running this ad." Laney tossed the small weekly newspaper on her desk and grimaced at her friend. "How can you eat when I have to go on the auction block?"

"Like this." Caro grinned as she bit into her sandwich.

Laney glared at Caroline. They'd agreed to meet at the office for lunch since neither had extra time nor money to go to restaurants on a regular basis.

"So you're going to do it?" Caro popped a shred of lettuce in her mouth.

"I guess so. It's a chance to get out of the gig I've had for the past couple of years. And if I don't do it—"

"You'll be in the morgue forever." Caro glanced out

17

of the corner of her eye at Laney and edged away slightly. "I think it's a good idea. You might meet someone."

"Like this guy? 'I like long walks along the pier and the smell of fresh fish and salt air.' We live in instate Georgia, for Pete's sake. Why can't they tell the truth, like 'I want a woman who'll cook, clean, and treat me like a king without expecting anything in return?' At least the girl would know what to expect."

"Party pooper. Okay, let's get down to it. Now, how would I describe you?" Caro pulled a legal pad out of the pile of papers on Laney's desk and dug a pen out of her purse.

"Oh no you don't. You'll describe what I'm wearing in three paragraphs like your gala interviews. I can do this myself."

"You're a better writer, but you need to embellish, build yourself up for the guys." Caro held on to her notepad as Laney tried to pry it from her hands.

Laney snorted a laugh. "Like I'm trying to impress a guy?"

"Why shouldn't you?" Caro held a hand up before Laney could complain yet again about her lousy assignment. "Look. You complain all the time about not having a decent crop of guys to choose from. This will give it to you. *And* if you put forth a decent effort, you might find a guy you like."

"And telling the truth's a bad thing?" Laney chuckled. "I knew you were good, but you have this dating thing down to a science, don't you?"

"A girl has to approach it rationally. When you're trying to get a date, it can be tough, so you have to be just as strong. So? Are you going to go for it and try to win a hunk?"

Laney quelled her need to run at the thought and waved a hand. "Okay, do it."

"Great. Let's see." Caro chewed on the end of her pen before writing with a beaming smile. " 'Striking, witty single woman seeking lone wolf.' That should do it for a headline."

"Oh man. I think we've hit a new low." Laney groaned then broke into a chuckle. "Can you believe I'm doing this? The person voted most likely to be single for life in my senior year? Boy, did Mr. Wheaton pick the wrong person for this assignment."

"Maybe not." Caroline glanced over Laney's shoulder with a flirtatious look. Laney suppressed a groan. Only one person worked at the paper who could bring that gleam to her friend's eyes. Caroline, along with half the female staff at *The Globe,* had a thing for Grant.

Laney turned to eye her new partner in crime. Across the room, he slouched in his chair, glaring at his computer monitor. What was he doing, planning her demise? Sure, he resented having to work with her, but what did he think of her writing? Of her? *Worry about the writing, Morgan. Not of his opinion of you.*

She succeeded in wresting the pad from Caro and got down to business. "We'd better get the personals ad done. I have to do one for an online dating service too, and it'll be a long one. Hope you can come by after work. I'll need all the help I can get."

Before she left work that evening, Laney called her personals ad into *The Messenger,* the weekly newspaper popular with the eclectic set in the city. In thirty words or less the ad had to convey her attractiveness, wit, and charm. And it took both her skill and Caro's to come up with enough adjectives to describe her positively, without lying. By the day after tomorrow, her ad would be published and being read by dozens if not more men. *Help.*

The plan for the evening, completing a multipage questionnaire for the popular online dating service, loomed ahead. In an effort to avoid going home and meeting Caro, Laney chose to write her first entry in the The Single Life column.

Being single in the new millennium is scary. And meeting nice men? That's nigh on impossible. But hope springs eternal, so this writer's going to try to navigate the obstacle course we all face. And if I make any wrong turns? Well, you'll be there to witness the show.

Grant sipped his morning coffee as he read through his first 'he said' installment for the column. That The Single Life would be a different slant on his past assignments was obvious, but whether he could remain impartial would be the question.

As a newspaper reporter, it's my job to investigate and observe objectively. Well, this assignment's a bit different than usual. For the next few weeks, I'll be the fly on the wall for my partner's dates. From a man's point of view, how does it look from the outside of the dating scene, looking in? I hope we all survive.

"Did you get the online questionnaire finished?" Caro sounded sleepy over the telephone.

"Where are you?" Laney grumbled as she stared at her monitor, trying to dredge up adjectives to describe her latest obit. How do you capsulize a life of over eighty years in twenty-five words or less?

"I had a fashion show to cover this morning, a breakfast event. Did you finish it? You still had three pages to go through when I left."

Laney rubbed her forehead. "Yeah. I finished it around two this morning and sent it to the website."

"When are you expected to be online?"

"The ad's supposed to make the website by the end of the week, maybe sooner, the e-mail said. And the newspaper ad will be out tomorrow." The wait, while a blessing, was also like sitting in the dentist's chair, all numbed and ready for the root canal. *Get it over with, already.*

"Well, we'll go through the answers when they start

coming in, okay?" Caro sounded more excited than Laney at the prospect.

"You don't have to help me, you know."

"I want to. Oh, got to go. The buffet is over and the show's starting." Caro broke the connection and Laney returned to the obits page. The rest of the morning she labored to make the pile in front of her dwindle.

"Hey, Delaney. Have you gotten online lately?"

Laney glanced up from her monitor to gaze at Grant as he strode toward her cubicle. The long list of obits she'd had to finish diminished throughout the day, though she'd worked through lunch and expected a late evening before she finished.

She pushed her chair away from her desk, stretched her back and eyed Grant. He looked a little too cheerful for her tastes. "Not this afternoon, why?" Her suspicions rose with the widening of his grin.

"Just wondering. Thought you might have had some answer to your online ad."

"I'm not supposed to be posted on the website until later in the week." Laney frowned. *Oh no.* "Have you been to the website?"

"Yep." He bounced on his feet and grinned.

"Am I on it?"

"Yep." For a man who didn't want to work with her, he was getting way too much enjoyment out of this.

"Oh."

She returned to her work station and minimized the

word processing program. In the few moments it took her to sign online, Grant advanced into the cubicle and stationed himself by her desk.

She stared at her computer. Funny, she considered the machine almost a friend, her companion. Now it felt as if the thing was out to get her. Drawing a deep breath she located the website, and quickly signed on to her account. Oh, jeez. She grimaced at the number before her. Twelve men had sent e-mails in reply to her personal ad, and it had been online only seven hours. Twelve!

"Well?" To his benefit, Grant didn't peer over her shoulder but studied her from his vantage point, his smile diminished somewhat.

Laney glanced up at Grant. "I got an answer already."

"How many?"

"Twelve."

"Since this morning?" He raised an eyebrow.

"Yeah, what do they do, lay in wait like sharks or wolves or something?"

He chuckled, "Don't get too excited. The guys just want to meet a nice girl."

Laney studied him. Did he just pay her a compliment?

"You'll do. It's not that tough, you know." He grinned and she tamped down the urge to smack him with her dinosaur figurine. Instead she glanced back at the list.

"You don't have to choose one of them to meet," she groused.

"Yeah, but I get to help pick him out." He actually rubbed his hands together.

"Oh no you don't. If you pick out a date for me, I'll end up writing my column on the perils of dating a man three times my age."

He laughed and leaned forward to see her monitor. Laney jerked away, intensely aware of his proximity. Why'd it matter? He'd been in her cubicle before, but now, even more than ever, he took her breath.

"Okay, if you insist on being in on this, let's use a bigger place." She shoved lightly at his shoulder, prompting him to straighten. They walked to his area and she sighed at the expanse.

"I wish I had as much room as you do. Why don't you have a cubicle, by the way?" She surveyed his working space. A large, L-shaped desk covered as much room as her entire cubicle encompassed, but he also had a couple of chairs, two filing cabinets and a long table. These pieces, though boundaries of his area, kept the space airy and open.

"I don't like feeling hemmed in. Okay, let's get to this. What's your password?" He opened the Internet window and looked at her expectantly.

"Uh uh. Let me." She strode to the desk and quickly logged in to the e-mail account she'd set up for the assignment. He scooted his chair over and pulled one close for her. Laney sat, aware of his lingering cologne after he'd removed his hand. Or was it just him?

"Okay, let's see. First we save all twelve of them to

the hard drive, then we'll cull." He made short work of the process, his gaze intent on the ads.

"Cull? Like culling a herd?" Laney scoffed. "There aren't that many to start with."

"And only after one day of an ad. Besides, all you need is one." He highlighted several paragraphs in the larger collection. "Let's get rid of the men twice your age."

Laney punched the delete button before he could and grinned impishly at him. She then leaned forward to scan the other replies.

"I don't mean to sound snobbish, but can we get rid of the ones who can't spell or make complete sentences?"

"Done. No awkward spellers allowed." And he deleted four more.

They read over the rest in silence for several minutes and pushed the delete button once more. Finally, they eyed each other. The two remaining e-mails were virtually alike. Both men liked to do things outdoors, talked of their kindness to animals and small children, and wanted a lasting relationship.

"Okay, now what?" Laney eyed the monitor. Neither man included a photo, so that didn't factor in. She bit her lip in thought.

"There's nothing to distinguish between the two ads." Grant leaned back in his chair and folded his hands over his flat stomach. "How do we use a scientific approach to pick one when they could be twins?"

Laney groaned, "Like this." She closed her eyes and pointed toward the screen. "That one."

"Hmm, random but workable."

She leaned forward and typed an innocuous e-mail and tried to be as positive as possible, all the while hoping the guy on the other side of the e-mail had already met the woman he'd spend the rest of his life with, small kids and pets included.

When she hit the send button she straightened away from Grant's computer to find him staring at her. "What?"

"Nothing. Other than the fact that we've started working together, and it hasn't been as bad as I thought. Good work, Lois."

"Lois?"

"Yeah, as in Clark and Lois."

She grinned at the play on Wheaton's remark. "Don't expect me to call you Superman."

"Well, good work anyway."

"Thanks." Laney cursed the blush she felt rising in her cheeks. How simple words like 'it wasn't bad' could make her feel warm inside was beyond her. But, coming from Grant, it was a high compliment.

Before he went home that evening, Laney intercepted Grant on the way to the coffee machine. "I got a reply from George, the online guy."

"Already?"

"Uh huh. And he wants to meet me for coffee. This evening." The panicked look in her eyes, something he could understand, compelled him to reassure her the only way he knew how, to get to the point of business.

"Okay, let's get the show on the road. When and where are you meeting?" He changed directions and headed for his desk to retrieve his briefcase.

"Sid's Coffee House in an hour."

Good decision. The local watering hole, a few minutes away, stayed busy throughout the day and into the evening.

"Let me leave first, I want to be there before you."

Laney smiled. "I'll be okay, you know. It's a public place."

"Yeah, but I'm still leaving the office first." A coffee house may be public, but she still would be meeting a stranger. Grant didn't stop to examine his new protective nature as he gathered his briefcase and suit coat.

He spent the drive to the coffee house in thought. The potential excitement factor for this assignment was mind-numbing. But maybe there would be a way to pull some benefit out of it.

The small coffee house, only ten minutes from the office, served as a meeting place as well as a restaurant. Grant frowned in confusion at the assortment of coffees offered before asking for a single black. The clerk acted as if it was an offense to eschew the lattes, mochas, and syrupy flavorings, but Grant didn't need more than a strong dose of caffeine. He carried the drink to a small table and took his notes out.

The list of prospective employers before him, compiled after a few phone calls and e-mails to friends in the business, served as a good start on making a change. And the leads were sure hits. The editorial position in Charlotte looked good, if he wanted to go that route. Then again, the national beat in Chicago might be a nice change. He grinned at the paper in front of him. Choices. Life was finally getting good. As long as he could keep Wheaton unaware he'd be fine. And Wheaton didn't much care about anything in the paper if he ended up looking good at the end of things.

Now, back to reality. He tucked the list into the back of his pad and leaned forward. Laney sat at the neighboring table of the coffee shop, just in his line of vision. She wore a flirty little dress, blue with tiny flowers on it. She must have gone home and changed first, but he didn't know how she'd managed to look so fresh. The dress, along with strappy sandals made her look appealing. Too young, too innocent for the dating game they were entering.

She sat quietly, though he knew she wanted to fidget. *He* wanted to fidget for her. And that stung, his feeling of empathy. He didn't want to feel sorry for her or put himself in her shoes.

The other side of the table was empty, had been for half an hour. Not a good sign. If the guy wanted to impress Laney, he was off to a bad start.

After a few minutes of inactivity, both on his part and at Morgan's table, it got to be too much. She looked way too lonely and Grant rose. His first step faltered as a middle-aged man, hair combed over to one side to hide his balding head, approached Delaney.

Grant eased back into his chair and watched her reaction. If she was disappointed, she managed to hide it well. Grant felt odd eavesdropping, but at least now, it was his job.

"Hi, are you Delaney?"

"I am. George?"

"That's me." George plopped down into the chair opposite Delaney and leaned toward her. Grant hid a grin and jotted down a note: *Don't come on too strong on your first date. You might scare her off.*

"So. What do you say we get this thing started?" George smiled and patted the hand Delaney rested on the tabletop. She slid it out from beneath his hold and swiped it on the skirt of her dress, out of sight of her date but in clear view of Grant. Poor kid. What a way to kick things off. Grant caught her eye and sent a wink her way. Funny thing, he wanted to reassure her she wasn't alone. And if he got a dig in, so much the better.

"I'm not sure I know what you mean; do you want to know something about me?" She was trying, Grant had to give her that.

"Nah. I know enough. You're pretty, got a good shape, and all your teeth." Combover laughed and almost fell on the tabletop in his attempt to get closer to her.

"And you?" Laney sipped at her coffee and Grant jotted another note for his column:

It's a good idea to have something to appear occupied with during a date. Coffee to drink, food to eat, a magazine to hide behind.

"Best teeth money can buy. Unattached and looking for some fun. So, what do you say? Want to hit a bar or two?"

"Um, sorry. I can't this evening. Work, you know." Laney hedged, edging away from the guy. At this rate, she was going to tilt her chair backwards, Grant mused.

"So give me your number and I'll call you. Set up another time."

"Why don't you give me *your* number?" Her smile could have frozen fresh-churned yogurt.

Combover babbled on, trying to cajole Laney into more dates or her telephone number. To give her credit, she smiled throughout and didn't give in. Instead, she tried to engage him in conversation then gave up and hid behind her coffee cup.

Grant slouched into his chair and doodled on the margins of the notepad. This was going to be a long date, for both of them. He might as well jot down some thoughts for tomorrow's column. He pulled the legal pad closer and started writing.

Being a fly on the wall can offer a lot of insight, as well as food for thought. Women have to take a lot from us, you know? Lines, pushy moments, and unfortunate choices in clothing or haircuts. Makes me think women are more courageous than men, agreeing to spend several hours with a complete stranger.

When she got home that evening Laney spent a half-hour in the shower, but the scent George had worn lingered in her brain. She sat at her laptop and hammered out an entry for the column while her thoughts were still fresh.

The date wouldn't rate as one of her most exciting, but it wasn't too bad. The knowledge that Grant was around had been embarrassing and comforting at the same time. And the wink. She grinned and tried to suppress the tendril of warmth from the memory of his half-cocked smile.

Body language. It's a powerful thing. When you go out for the first time, it's important not to smile too much, lean forward too far, or cross your arms over your chest. It might give the wrong impression. But body language can be a good thing too. It can give you a lot of information, without saying a word. And it can be a great weapon in the battle of the sexes.

Chapter Three

"**H**ello." Laney tucked her cell phone between her shoulder and neck and opened her file cabinet. She'd stored notes for her online dating research somewhere—

"Delaney? This is Todd. From *The Messenger* personals ad?"

She sank into her chair and clutched the phone tighter. In the last three days, she'd met George, answered another ad online, and talked with two guys from the weekly newspaper ad. *It's all for business, just like interviewing jail inmates.*

"Hi, Todd. How are you?"

"Good, good. I wanted to call and talk, maybe set up a time to meet." At least this guy sounded nice.

"Okay. Well, why don't you tell me a little about

yourself first? That way we'll know if we're compatible." *Please don't be like the other guy from the personals. Who knew there were still people who didn't believe men landed on the moon?* At least she'd found out before meeting him. Thank heavens for Caro's tips on interviewing potential dates.

"Well, let's see." Todd talked for a few minutes and Laney reciprocated with pertinent information. Surprisingly, he sounded like someone she could like. Normal, even. Laney glanced toward her editor's office. Through the open door, he could be seen in conversation with Grant.

"So, you've heard the worst, still want to meet?" Todd's playful tone invited her to respond in kind.

Laney laughed and assented. In no time they agreed to meet at Sid's for a late lunch that day. At the rate she was using his place, Sid was going to start charging her rent.

She hung up and returned to her research of the singles scene in the area. *Man, there's a lot of lonely people out there.*

"Find me a date, will ya?" Caroline slumped into the chair alongside Laney's desk, rummaging through her pockets at the same time.

Laney grinned. "Can't find your cigarettes?"

"Gave them up. Now I'm stuck eating sugar-free mints, thanks to you."

"It does cause more wrinkles, you know." Laney grinned.

"Yeah, but gaining weight would bankrupt me. I'd have to buy a whole new wardrobe."

Laney envied her friend's style, as well as her poise. "Why do you need a date? You've never had a problem finding guys. And God knows you have the ins on finding out about men before you go out with them."

"That was before I broke up with Chad." Caro located a tube of mints and offered Laney one.

"Chad? Which one was he?"

"The guy from the video store. The one renting the chick flicks."

"Oh, yeah. Why'd you break up?"

Caroline shrugged. "He was a sensitive guy. Too sensitive. I got tired when he cried at every movie we saw."

Laney giggled. "We should have known. But you don't need help meeting guys. You seem to have them crawling out of the woodwork."

"Yeah, but who wants termites?" Caroline popped a mint into her mouth. "What about you? Got any prospects?"

"Maybe. There's this one guy . . ."

The coffee shop's lunch crowd had dropped off to a few tables' worth of diehard drinkers by the time Laney arrived for her date with Todd. She glanced around the restaurant and spied Grant idly scanning the newspaper while he sipped a mug of coffee. *Bet he took it black. No mocha lattes for Grant Stone, no sir.*

She stood in the alcove and waited. Todd's description of himself, tall, thin, and blond, was general, but she didn't see anyone that would fit the description. No, wait. There, there was the white shirt and flag lapel pin. Oh goodie, and a pocket protector.

He stood diffidently, almost hidden by a hanging plant near the creamery station. Laney smiled encouragingly. She didn't want to approach him, just meeting was forward enough. Still, he stood, his hands folded in front of him, only making eye contact with her briefly.

Finally, Laney gathered her courage and advanced. "Todd?"

He smiled and nodded. No voice, though.

She held her smile with some effort. This was going to hurt. "So, should we get some coffee and find a table?"

Silently he gestured that she should precede him, and Laney went to the counter to place her order.

Grant smothered a chuckle. Poor Morgan. In the space of an hour and a half her date hadn't uttered a word without being prompted. Not once. Just listening to the one-sided conversation made Grant yawn. And he didn't have to focus on making conversation for two.

What would she do if she got a decent guy on one of these outings? If the kid talked, he might stand a chance of taking her home, Grant mused. And then what? Would they share a sweet good night kiss? And would he have to watch? Somehow, the idea of seeing Laney kiss this bum good night was more disturbing than just the notion of being a voyeur.

After several blank moments, Todd finally glanced at his watch and made his excuses. Laney's smile stayed plastered on until he exited the building. Then her head hit the table.

Grant stood and approached her. "Hey, Lois."

"Where's Superman when I need him?" she mumbled into the tabletop before raising her head.

Grant slid out the chair abandoned by her date and turned it around before straddling it. "That looked painful."

"You have no idea." She rubbed the center of her forehead.

"Headache?"

"Splitting. I need caffeine and an aspirin, in that order."

"I can't help with the aspirin, but coffee I can do. What do you want?"

"Caramel mochiato. Largest one they have. And a large slice of chocolate cake." Her smile was grateful as she fumbled in her purse, presumably for the medication.

Grant placed the order at the counter and waited impatiently for her coffee and dessert. He refilled his own before joining her. She accepted the coffee with murmured thanks. *She's a pretty little thing, when she's not talking so much.*

"So. Prince Charming?" He sat opposite her at the table. She sipped the hot drink then with a sigh sliced into the cake, though the thing looked more like chocolate fudge with icing on it. Whatever, though, she looked less stressed after one bite. The scent of caramel, chocolate, and flowers combined in a compelling flavor—that was Laney.

Morgan grimaced. "Ugh. If he'd talked, maybe I could tell you whether I liked him or not. The way it stands, I know he's an accountant, unmarried, and lives north of the city. I felt like a marionette master."

"Not a big talker, agreed. But, he's gainfully employed, doesn't live with his mother. Two points in his favor, I'd say."

"Very funny." Laney leaned back in her chair, boneless in her sprawl. "I'm exhausted. Who would think one date could be so tiring?"

"Well, two down. Only what? Seven more to go?"

She glanced at her watch. "Nooo. I'm going home. Take a bath. Forget I have to talk to anyone."

"I'll walk you out." He stood and tossed the remains of their coffees in the trash.

"Why?" Delaney arched a look toward him as they exited into the sunlit afternoon.

"No reason." He tugged the sleeves of his jacket down, avoiding her eyes.

"You're making sure I get to my car all right, aren't you, Clark?" She grinned.

"So? You never know with guys nowadays, and my blue spandex suit is in the cleaners." Grant glanced around. No skinny blond guy lurking behind the bushes.

Laney strode ahead of him toward her car. "Be careful, Stone. I might start to think you're human after all."

Once home, Laney wrote a short excerpt for her column before showering and planting herself in front of the television, ready for a Hitchcock retrospective. And determined not to think of how handsome Grant Stone had been at the café today.

First impressions. In dating, they're everything. Deciding what to wear, how much to disclose when you're chatting with your date, even how you sit has an impact on whether you get asked out again. All in all, it's a wonder anyone ever connects. One piece of advice, though. Talk. No matter what about, please keep up your end of the conversation. To carry on a one-sided tête-à-tête is too painful to do all on your own.

That evening, Grant channel-surfed through ballgames and replays of golf matches before settling on the classic movie channel and a murder mystery. With the television playing in the background, he wrote his column.

Rules of dating. Seems simple, right? Be polite, wear clean socks, and refrain from belching in public. But there are more rules, at least for the woman. Don't go on a date with a stranger unless it's in a public place. At the end of the date, make sure you go to a well-lit parking

"God, I sound like someone's father." Grant groaned and repeatedly hit the delete button.

in a public place. Finally, smile casually, but not too invitingly. You might get more than you bargain for.

He saved the column onto the hard drive of his laptop. Whether he used it or not was up in the air. Too much of his own feelings of protectiveness were starting to float to the surface with this whole business, and that had to stop.

Chapter Four

"I knew this would be a good column. Three weeks into the thing and look at these numbers."

Grant sat beside Laney in Wheaton's office and tried not to notice her hair. What had seemed like a childish style a few weeks ago now suited her perfectly, and framed her delicate features. This had to stop, he reminded himself.

In the last week he'd fielded two telephone interviews from Baton Rouge and Des Moines. For various reasons, they didn't suit, but that didn't mean he would stay at *The Globe*. He had to leave the paper as soon as he could find a better job. Now wasn't the time to become involved with anyone. But could he leave the column before finishing the column's run? To do so might hurt his reputation for bringing in the story, no matter what.

Grant eyed the city editor with a sense of foreboding. "What are the demographics?"

"That's the great part of the whole thing. We're up across the board in the first month. I thought the twenty-five-to-thirty-year-old female population would bite, but every adult demographic under sixty-five is expressing interest."

"So, we continue with the column." Laney fidgeted in her chair.

"You bet you do. And your plans are great. Keep up the good work, guys."

"Have there been any negative responses?" Grant leaned forward to glance at the report on Wheaton's desk.

The editor waved a hand dismissively. "Not enough to count. I tell you, this is a gold mine. You two are perfect for the column."

He crowed for a few more minutes, not allowing either Laney or Grant to make any critical comments. Instead, he planned the rest of the excursions they'd have to live through. Just what his career needed, Grant steamed. A reputation as a paid escort for a newspaper-sanctioned dating service.

Wheaton dismissed them by turning his attention to other papers on his desk, essentially ignoring them. Grant stalked to his desk space and flopped into his chair. Why was he so angry? The column *was* going well. Even the guys at his gym commented on it, albeit in a joking manner. If circulation increased as a result of their work, both he and Laney would have more to bargain with in job searches and assignments. But the notion of going out with her, yet not dating Laney stuck in his craw.

Laney passed him on the way to her cubicle, another pile of death notices clutched in her hand. Her muttered question filtered to him as she strode past his desk: "If I have such a popular column, why do I have to keep doing the obits?"

"Still have to pay the piper, Morgan." Grant stood and picked up his coffee mug, intent on getting a fresh cup.

Her expressive eyes blazing with frustration, she whirled around and trailed him to the coffee station. "And dating by assignment isn't payment enough?"

He grunted at the sight of an empty carafe. "Try hanging out in an alley waiting for a tip. Or showing up at a burning house right after the fire department. Or—"

"You love it. And those are the stories *I* want to do. The stories that make a difference." Laney held up the brownish-stained coffee decanter and grimaced.

"You and every other reporter in the office. There aren't enough to go around, you know. You want to go get a cup of coffee?"

"Why not make another pot? Though I'd never drink this stuff."

"Why? Coffee's coffee."

"Wait 'til we get to the coffee shop, then you'll see what real coffee tastes like."

"So get your stuff, Lois. I need a break." He gave her a nudge toward her desk and belongings.

They hustled out of the office and drove the short distance to Sid's coffee shop. Grant stared at the menu in disbelief. "How can one beverage be so confusing?"

Laney giggled. "That's why you get it black?"

"Yeah. There are too many lattes, cappus, and syrups to figure out. Besides, all I need is a solid hit of caffeine during the day."

"I can still get you that, with flavor." Laney turned and ordered for both of them. Grant grinned at her enthusiasm. Who knew ordering a cup of coffee could be so entertaining?

They waited for what looked like a performance in a Japanese grill. But rather than slicing and dicing vegetables the coffee clerk brewed and steamed, stirred and frothed with meticulous care. Finally, after an eternity of breathing in tantalizing aromas, the clerk presented several mugs with little flourish.

Laney handed him two steaming cups with a grin and gathered two more. "I'm going to convert you, just watch and see."

He eyed the froth on top of one cup with some caution. "I hope so. What's in them?"

"No kryptonite, I promise. Don't complain. Everything that's good is worth a little work." She led

the way to what had become his usual table for recon-
noitering and sat. "Try them first, then I'll tell you
what's in each."

He had to admit, the coffees smelled good, much
better than the brew he managed to put together each
morning at his house. He chose a small cup of hot,
black coffee; at least it resembled his own a little.

The burst of flavor surprised him and he lifted his
gaze to Laney's. "Good."

"It's a Sumatran blend espresso. Has a lot of body, a
little spicy flavor. I kind of thought that would suit
you." Her cheeks pinkened and she gestured toward
another cup. "Try that one."

"What's on top?"

"A froth of milk, that's all."

Grant eyed the puffy, slightly melted topping.
"Milk's supposed to mix in the coffee, not stay on top
of it."

Laney laughed. "Just try it."

He took a drink and wiped his mouth free of milk
with a napkin. "It's okay, not as good as the first one."

"I figured you wouldn't like it, it's a little too sweet
with the vanilla syrup. It's a vanilla latte, incidentally.
Espresso with a shot of vanilla syrup and milk. Now,
for the last one." She slid another mug toward him.

Grant tasted the brew and gave it a nod, the espresso
might be just the thing first thing in the morning, but
without the milk. He grinned at her and nodded to the
cup she held. "What about that one?"

"That's mine."

"So? Too sweet?"

Laney shook her head and offered the mug. He should have known. The essence of cinnamon and something more, orange maybe, permeated the coffee, with a sweetness he found both attractive and appealing. The coffee suited her. He returned it after a cautious sip.

"So? Did you like it?"

He shrugged. "It's good, but has a little too much flavor if you know what I mean."

Laney grinned. "I know. You're a black coffee kind of guy. But you have to agree, this is much better than that sludge you're used to in the office." She gestured to the plain espresso.

He nodded and sipped before returning to the main reason for the outing. "You okay with continuing the column?"

"I guess." She shrugged. "I'd rather prove myself with something more relevant but if this is it, this is it."

"Look at it this way, there's only so many good stories out there. You have to win them the hard way, if it's going to count." Grant drank the Sumatran coffee. It wasn't half bad.

"So, this whole thing is a race."

"Yeah. And someone's got to win. Might as well be us."

"Us?" She cocked her head at him, a curl draping over her ear in a caress.

"It's why I'm doing the dating column, Lois. Same as you."

"I thought we were competing."

"Not for the job, but maybe for the career. Want a refill?" He went to stand in line. Another Sumatran would come in handy.

That afternoon, unwilling to face the newsroom and the prospect of facing the singles column, Laney begged Caroline to meet her for a much needed break, and waited for her at the coffee shop. She'd enjoyed her time with Grant today, too much. The man who'd intimidated her in the past treated her like an equal. And worse, the attraction she'd tamped down when she worked with him as an intern, so long ago, returned full force.

Their coffees lasted another hour, then with little fanfare he'd left. His departure hit her with the realization that even though they'd buried the hatchet, it was still hanging over her head, waiting for any screwup.

"You're kidding. He admitted he was competing with you?" Caroline sipped her soda as Laney munched on her sandwich.

"Not in so many words. But if we continue to bring in good numbers and if a position on the city beat opens up . . ." Laney shrugged. "Who knows? I guess we are competing."

"Which makes for a weird working relationship."

"Yeah." Laney glanced over Caroline's shoulder and

groaned. Her friend glanced up from her salad with a questioning look. "What?"

"Remember the online guy?" Laney lowered her voice though he was at least a couple of yards away and facing the other direction.

"The one who wanted—"

"That's the one. He's at a table behind you." Laney stopped Caroline from turning to gawk. "Don't turn around, he might notice us. And believe me, you don't want his attention."

Caroline smiled slightly. "Do you want to leave?"

"No. I don't think he'll bother us."

Before her words faded he hovered over her table, his cologne announcing his presence.

"Hiya, sweet thing. How you doing?" With lines like that, he should have had gold chains dripping from his neck. Wait, was that a glint she saw? Nope, just sparse chest hair.

"So, you didn't call. You want to set a time to go out and have some fun?" He leaned forward, almost into her plate.

"No thanks."

"Aw, come on. We hit it off didn't we, Delia? Let's get to it. Maybe you can bring your friend here?" He eyed Caroline. The traitor scooted her chair a few feet away from the table.

"Nice offer, but no. Now, if you'll excuse us—"

George, or Combover, as Grant dubbed him, leaned closer, to the point she could count the individual strands covering his bald spot. "No, no, no. You don't understand. You have to get together—"

"She said no, mister. Now back off." A hand appeared on Combover's shoulder and pried him away. Combover whimpered, cursed, and railed against the rough treatment but eventually left, with the help of the manager and her rescuer.

Laney clasped her trembling hands on the table's surface. A combination of adrenaline and anger flowed through her, causing her stomach to churn.

"Are you okay?" Grant returned to their table and dropped down on his haunches beside her chair.

"What are you doing?" Laney pushed her food away and glared at him.

"Huh? What am I—"

"I was handling that jerk just fine, and you didn't have to get involved. And what are you doing back here, now?"

His eyes narrowed and he leaned toward her. "It didn't look like you were handling it. It looked like he was on the verge of manhandling you and your friend here."

"Caroline, nice to meet you." Caro pulled her seat forward into Grant's line of vision.

"Hi. You okay, did he harass you too?" He briefly glanced at Caroline.

"Only by proximity and cologne. Laney got the full treatment." Caroline smiled flirtatiously.

His gaze returned to Laney as she slid out of the chair and gathered her trash. "I'll walk you ladies to your car."

"Don't bother, we're fine." Laney threw her purse over her shoulder and headed to the exit, belatedly aware of how close that brought her to him.

"No bother." He opened the door for them. "And to answer your second question, we have to talk about the column."

"So talk."

"It can wait 'til we get to the office."

Oh, it'd wait until they got to the office, she fumed. And then she'd let him have it. Treating her like a poor little thing wasn't going to work. Especially not when it aroused warm tingly feelings in her stomach.

She parted ways with Caro at their cars and with a parting glare at Grant, stomped to her car.

"Problem?" At a loss, Grant glanced at Laney as she sat scowling.

Laney perched on the chair beside his desk, her brown eyes blazing, and her slender frame fairly quivering with ire.

"What was the meaning of all that?"

"All what?" As if he couldn't guess, but she was kind of cute when she was mad so he let it ride.

"All the macho stuff. 'I'll walk you to your car.' Walk my right elbow. You followed me all the way back to the office, and into the parking area."

"I was coming back to the office. Where else would I park?" Damn, but he enjoyed this.

"And you had to follow right on my bumper? I slowed down so you could pass me."

"Yeah, I noticed the twenty-five in a forty zone." He leaned back and crossed his hands behind his head.

"And you didn't take the hint?" Her voice rose to a higher pitch.

"I figured you just wanted to extend your lunch hour."

"Look, just do your job. And it doesn't include putting on your tights and cape, mister, so butt out of my business otherwise." Laney spit out the last, sprang from her chair, and pounced off.

"We need to talk about the column!" he yelled to her back before chuckling. "What'd I say?" He glanced around the newsroom with a grin.

"Angling for the man of the year award, Stone?" A female reporter he'd shared a few drinks with sauntered up to him. The fact he couldn't remember more about her was a good indication of how much she impressed him.

"Nah. Just joking around with my latest writing partner."

"I thought you worked best alone."

"Sometimes it's more fun with someone else." And as he headed to the break room to refill his coffee Grant realized he enjoyed just about everything about Delaney Morgan. Talking to her, baiting her, even drinking fancy coffee with her. Odd how what had started out as an onerous task could alter into something he enjoyed.

Only one thing bothered him. The annoying feeling of protectiveness that hit whenever he thought of that jerk hitting on her. Could be bad news, indeed, that feeling.

He refilled his coffee from the oldest carafe, the one with the permanent brown stains. He wouldn't drink it of course. Even he didn't have that much iron in his stomach. But he did need to talk to Laney about the next installment of their assignment. He had to find out if he could go with her on her next appointment to the matchmaker. And bringing the foul smelling stuff into contact with her sensitive palette would rile her more. Man this was fun.

"My goodness, you're precious."

Laney tried for a bright smile, but she managed only a sick grimace instead. "Thank you, Myra. How long have you been a matchmaker?"

She perched on a very uncomfortable sofa in a house that belonged in the last century, or make that the century before. Victorian furniture obviously wasn't meant to be rested on but looked at, because she was fast becoming numb from sitting on the horsehair couch.

"Since I was a teenager. Of course I've only been doing it for a living for the past ten years." Myra cast a curious glance toward Grant, who tried to blend in with the furniture.

"My ride. My car broke down this afternoon." Laney hated lying to the woman. But what other explanation would work? He was her bodyguard? Not believable, if you saw her car and clothes. Her chaperone? Not in this century. So, they'd come up with the idea of the car trouble. It wasn't too unbelievable, seeing as how she drove the ancient bug. It may be a classic and a collector's item, but it was still a pain in the neck getting repaired.

"Well, it's a bit unusual for the client to have company with them, but all the same, we can get started." Myra nodded to Grant, who managed to look more uncomfortable than Laney felt, if that was possible.

Her matchmaker managed to expel any image of a plump little lady surrounded by her cats that Laney envisioned. The spandex leopard print blouse Myra Lange sported with her tight black pants cast her in the role of a gangster's moll more than a grandmother. Even the high-heeled black slides matched, with a plastic leopard print bow showing off her scarlet tipped toes.

"How does this work?" Laney found the prospect of another person matching her with a date more intimidating than an impersonal computer or a personals column.

Myra indicated the clipboard she held in her hand. "I need to ask you some questions but don't worry. We'll talk mostly. Then, once we're clear on what you like in a mate and what you're looking for in a relationship, I'll get to work."

What she wanted in a relationship? Laney wasn't even sure she wanted a relationship with anyone at all, much less knowing what qualities in a man were important.

"You know that many people? Can match so many?"

"Of course. Now, let's get to it. Tell me about yourself. What do you do for a living?"

As she answered the questions, Laney dwelled on the ultimate question. What *did* she want in a mate? Did she even know? She mentally reviewed the men she'd dated in the past year or so. Dale, the contractor. All muscle and no thought. Kevin, the attorney. Intellect absent the emotion. As her mind ran through the men she had been on one date with, she inwardly groaned. Glory, she couldn't come up with one well-rounded guy in the whole bunch. All the time she answered the questions, though, she was aware of her silent witness. Grant learned far too much about her in this gig.

By the end of the two-hour session, Laney felt as if she'd sat through a session with a shrink or, in the alternative, with her mother. Myra delved into her psyche as surely as if she held an advanced degree.

"Honey, I'll have you hooked up with a wonderful guy before you know it. I'll give you a call in a couple of days."

Laney stood ready to flee in a panic, fearful that Myra just might do that. Grant slowly rose and advanced to meet her at the parlor door.

"I feel like I've been on a rack. How did people sit in

those chairs one hundred years ago?" He rubbed the back of his neck as they strode toward his car.

"I don't know," Laney answered absently, her mind still on the interview.

"You okay?"

"Yeah. Just thinking."

"About what?"

"Just about the questions she asked. I need to write an article about the whole process, and I want to remember some of the interview questions for my column."

Grant shook his head. "Well, if the amount of information she looked for is any indication, she should have you matched and married in a month."

Sure enough, two days later, Myra called and arranged for a meeting between Craig and Laney. The repeated scene of the crime, Sid's coffee shop, was the designated meeting place. When Laney entered she avoided the employees' gazes, sure they were placing bets on what kind of guy would show up. She buried herself behind a book at her table to quell anyone with suggestions, like she'd done at lunch the other day.

Out of the corner of her eye, she saw Grant sit at the table, a cup of coffee and Danish in front of him. Why hadn't she thought of food? She could use a chocolate muffin right now.

"Hi, Laney?"

"Hi." Laney smiled up from her book. The man standing before her had the look of a blond athlete, trim and energetic. He wore a polo shirt and jeans but managed to emanate an air of fashion Grant never managed to pull off, even when dressed in a nice suit. Now, where did that come from? Laney mentally shrugged off the thought.

He introduced himself as Craig and accepted her invitation to sit. Cute, blond, and fit, with a nice smile, she thought. A decent start.

"Myra sends her regards." He smiled encouragingly. "She mentioned that you work at a newspaper?"

Laney relaxed into the conversation. Within minutes she learned more about Craig than any man so far. And as the afternoon progressed, she realized she was having a good time.

She laughed at Craig's joke and responded with a quip of her own, mildly amazed that she wanted to continue the conversation. All along, though, the image of a scowling Grant, seated at a nearby table, filled her periphery.

Grant frowned into his coffee. Laney's current assignment, working with a matchmaker, had started out as a laugh for him, until he sat in on the interview. Witnessing the interview and conversation between Laney and Myra a couple of days ago brought home the intrusive nature of being a reporter. Laney's life had opened up to him. And she hadn't lied in answer to the questions, she'd taken them seriously. How he knew that, he wasn't sure, but he knew.

The more he followed her, watched her, the more convinced Grant became that Laney didn't realize the danger she, indeed every single woman, put herself in, at least emotionally. Meeting a guy who'd appreciate her humor, her quirky way of looking at things, her weird obsession with coffee, would be a tall order. Surely there were better ways for a nice girl to meet a man than online, on the phone, or through a matchmaker. Even if she was on assignment, it didn't look as if Laney met guys other than through her job. Maybe he could fix—No. He didn't know any nice men, and the idea of fixing her up with men he did associate with left him cold.

This guy didn't look so bad. He hadn't made a pass in the last thirty minutes, kept her attention by all accounts, and even made her laugh. So would she find him okay? If she dated someone more than once it would be great for the column, for his career. So why wasn't it more satisfying?

"Is Friday night a good time for you?" Craig offered, his gaze admiring.

"Could I let you know?" Laney hedged, not sure why. She had no plans for Friday night, other than her laundry and watching pay per view. Yet, she wasn't sure about seeing Craig again.

"Okay. Here's my number. Give me a call." He laid his business card on the table. "I really do want to see you again, Laney."

"It's been great meeting you." Laney extended her hand. After a warm clasp, Craig left. She rose and went to the coffee bar for a much needed latté refill.

She returned to the table to find Grant settled there. His coffee cup was full to the brim and steaming, indicating his intent to stay a while. She hid a smile at the aroma of the coffee. A Sumatran blend.

"Time for a review of the evening," he announced before she could sit.

"I'm not sure I want to review the evening right now, thanks."

"Why? He didn't molest you, didn't make any rude comments or spill his food on you. You didn't have to speak for him. Should've been a snap." Grant leaned back in his chair and crossed an ankle over his knee.

"That's why, I guess. I need to analyze what happened, figure out what to say in the column."

"If you talk about it, it'll be more lucid. Cleaner."

Laney chuckled dryly. "I've talked more in the past couple of hours than in the last week. No, let me rephrase. I've talked more in the past week, what with Myra and Craig, than in the past month. Man, am I tired of talking."

"So, let's not talk. Let's go for a ride." Grant stood and strode to the counter, returning with two foam cups and lids. He quickly poured their coffees into the containers and sealed them. Laney stared, openmouthed, as he cleared away the rest of the clutter from the table. "Are you coming?"

"Where?"

"I told you, a drive. We both need a break from dating, watching dating, talking about dating—"

Laney laughed, her mood lightened. It was a relief to delay dealing with her emotions. "Fine, let's go."

The gleaming silver Corvette, crouched in its parking space, made all of the SUVs, sedans and minivans dull in comparison. Grant ran a palm over the roof as he unlocked and opened Laney's door. "Let it cool off first, it can be an oven."

He rounded the hood and opened his door then leaned in and turned the ignition. After he'd flipped on the air conditioning, he straightened and leaned his elbows on the hot roof. "Want country or city?"

"Country. I need to relax."

"Yeah. Dating all those men can be exhausting, I'm sure." With a smirk he motioned for her to climb into the car. She edged onto the leather seat, expecting it to be flaming hot. Instead, the deep red upholstery felt supple and only slightly warm. The low passenger seat surrounded her and molded to her shape. Talk about relaxing, she thought. An hour or two of this and some slow calming music would do the trick.

Once in his car, Laney slumped down in her seat and surreptitiously slipped off her shoes. "You know, Stone. We may not agree on a lot of things, but this car is prime."

"Thanks. I like it. It was the one thing I insisted on

keeping in the divorce." His eyes were on the sunset-lit road, his expression set.

"You were married?" She realized she knew nothing about him. And it wasn't fair, since he'd heard her life, complete with love stories, a few days ago.

"For about five years."

"What happened?"

Grant shrugged and downshifted as he exited the interstate. "She got tired of me, I guess. Found someone she was more interested in."

"Her loss."

"Yeah, right. Just goes to show there's no such thing as fidelity. No point in getting married. If you're going to get bored after a few years, no point in binding yourself to another person legally."

Grant's voice faded, as if he was embarrassed at his disclosure.

Laney shifted her gaze to the side of the road, letting the scenery slide by. "I disagree."

"About what? Marriage or fidelity?"

"Both. My parents have been married for over thirty years and their marriage is firm, so is my grandparents'. And if you love someone, really love someone, you're going to be there for the long haul."

"No wonder you've never found anyone for a long-term relationship, Morgan. You're lost in fairyland. Or the romance aisle of the bookstore."

Laney turned in her seat, ignoring the calm of the

rural Georgia roads. "It's not unrealistic to expect someone to love you. What's sad is when you give up. And clearly you have."

"I haven't given up on companionship and all that. I've just become more pragmatic." He took a turn onto an even more pastoral lane. "Want some peaches? There's a couple of farm stands up ahead."

"No, I don't want peaches, besides they'd be closed at this hour. Look, I met a nice guy this afternoon. Why shouldn't I think about seeing Craig again? Establishing a relationship with him?"

"No reason. Just go in with your eyes open. Don't expect happily ever after to last more than a couple of years." He took a sip of his coffee and grimaced. "Cold."

"Yeah, like you," Laney huffed. "Look, why are we talking about Craig like he's my one true love? He's a nice guy. That's all."

"Wait a while. You'll find out he wears unmatched socks, or brushes his teeth with a toothpaste you don't like, or something equally important."

"You are so—"

"Truthful? Down to earth? Practical?"

"Cynical, scornful. Half-empty." She glanced around her. "I think I do want some peaches. That gas station ahead has a sign they sell them. Pull over there."

She needed a break. From him, from his scorn of a state she craved, from the reality of her life.

She bought peaches she didn't want, he bought cof-

fee he didn't drink, and they headed back to the coffee shop and her car, the light mood they'd sought
evaporated.

The next morning Laney tried to put into words her
ambiguity toward Craig, Grant, and the whole male
population.

*What happens when you meet someone who's per-
fectly nice? I wonder. Nice looks, nice jokes, nice
everything. The larger question, I suppose, is
whether you can connect with the person. Even if
everything seems above board and perfectly fine,
if you can't relate emotionally, even physically
with the man, being nice and meeting nice isn't
enough. Is it?*

Grant could make out Laney from his desk, her short
curls framing her face as she studiously typed. How
unrealistic could she get? Only kids had the kind of
wide-eyed wonder she did and she was in her twenties,
for crying out loud. She needed a keeper.

Unfortunately, it looked like he had the assignment.

*What's a woman looking for in a man?
Compliments? Truthfulness? A good job? Or is
she looking for something that's impossible to
generate? When a man goes out on a date, his pri-
mary goal is to impress. Let's face it, guys, we'll
say almost anything to get to the next step, the next*

date. Is that fair? And how do we know the lady isn't stretching the truth as well? What face do we show when we're trying to find the love of our life? And if we're lying to the lady, aren't we lying to ourselves?

Chapter Five

The pile of home and business correspondence on his desk threatened to topple when Grant shifted, after filing his column. He grimaced, it was time he went through the stuff. After fifteen minutes of organizing the mail into keep, toss, and respond piles, he dumped the useless paper into the trash and went through the pertinent.

An offer for an editorship in Charlotte. Hmm, looked good. He'd call in a few days and set up an interview. Or e-mail, maybe.

The Chicago opening looked interesting. A city beat position. Could develop into something more, maybe national or international. It was more than interesting. It looked really good. Grant glanced at the telephone number then pulled his cell phone from his pocket and dialed. With the chaos of a busy newsroom, he was sure he wouldn't be overheard. After a minute's chat with the Chicago editor, he set up a time for a telephone interview and then got to work.

Laney's dating had gone well, but it wasn't over yet. They had another facet of singles life to investigate, the fast date.

"You've got a message, Laney. You might want to check it before you take lunch." The receptionist at the front of the newsroom handed Laney a slip of paper.

She halted her progress out of the office and took a cursory glance at the note.

Caroline stood by, her designer handbag draped elegantly over her linen jacket-covered shoulder. "Do you need to deal with that?"

"No, I'll call after we eat." Laney tucked the note inside a pocket in her own purse and continued toward the door.

"You sure?"

"Yeah. It's just something about the The Single Life column. From Craig."

Caroline held her silence as they headed for the elevator then sighed in exasperation. "The guy you thought was nice? He's the one that had possibility, wasn't he?"

"I guess. But this is a job, Caro, nothing more."

"A job. Right. Do you want to go to the coffee shop or somewhere else for lunch?"

Over their food, Laney started to outline the next area she had to investigate. Caro interrupted her with questions about Craig until she quelled her with a look.

"I haven't decided on whether I want to see him again, Caro. And nothing you say or ask or hint at will make my decision any faster."

Caro sipped her iced tea. "Fine. I just want you to consider this. If you'd met Craig a month ago, would you have hesitated to go out with him? And why are you hesitating now?"

The image of Craig at the coffee shop rose in her mind, quickly followed by a picture of Grant as they sped in the country lanes in his car. Was he the reason she hesitated with Craig? And if he was, did she want to admit the attraction to Caro or even to herself?

She avoided the topic and returned to the next assignment she had as part of the singles column.

"Fast Date?" Caro looked intrigued and uncomfortable at the same time.

"Uh huh. I'm supposed to go to this restaurant's private dining room, talk to ten or fifteen guys and see if we click."

"So? Sounds like a mixer to me. No different than in college."

Laney grimaced at the thought of the parties Caro dragged her to, both in college and after, in hopes of meeting Mr. Right. "Well, this is different. You have up to ten minutes with each guy and have to find out if you're interested in them within that time period."

"Yuck. Sounds like glorified job interviews to me." Caro shuddered melodramatically.

"Right. And we know how comfortable those are."

"Welcome to Fast Date. We're going to have fun to-night folks, so let's get started." The host and hostess of the dating event smiled blindingly, as if they could beam the fidgety crowd their confidence.

"Think of the fast date as a quick snapshot of a longer date. Put your best foot forward and be friendly. Convince the other person you're worth getting to know," the woman chirped, as if that didn't put the fear of God into every soul in the private dining room of the restaurant. Laney thought back to Caro's comments about the job interviews. Fast Date was shaping up to rank right up there with root canals and first dates.

Laney and Grant stood a few feet apart, chatting with members of their own sex, much like a junior high dance. In order for him to observe without making him-self too noticeable, Grant had to agree to participate in the ten-minute fast dating event, something that sent Laney into giggles. Just the sight of Grant filling out the attraction inventory alongside her was comical, as was his expression.

She held her nametag in her hand, along with her assigned table number. Soon the process of job inter-view after job interview would begin. *Help.*

"Okay, ladies and gentlemen. We're ready to go. Ladies, find the table your number corresponds to and have a seat. Gentlemen, you also have a number assigned to you. That's the table you'll start at. Have a seat and then we'll explain further."

The room shuffled and scattered until there was a couple at each small table, the occupants either checking each other out or avoiding eye contact altogether.

The host actually rubbed his hands together. "Now. You'll each have ten minutes to talk, get to know each other, and make a connection. At the end of ten minutes, a bell will sound and the gentlemen will move on to the next table. If you want to move from the table area during your ten-minute date, fine. Just remember to keep within the time frame."

The hostess continued. "At the end of the fast dating session, each of you will fill out the interest guide in your packet. Indicate which of the fast dates you'd like to see again. We'll take it from there. Ready? Begin."

Laney looked at the older gentleman across from her and plunged in. "Hi, I'm Laney."

Over the course of the evening she talked to an accountant, an attorney, and a house painter, along with others she couldn't remember. After a while the men blurred together, cloning into an amalgam of hobbies, preferences and smiles. All but one.

Grant held number seven of nineteen. Him, she remembered.

"Hey." He slumped into his chair. "Man, do I need a drink."

"So, they have a bar." She glanced over her shoulder

toward the end of the room, where two or three couples lined up at the counter, chatting and sipping.

"Yeah, but I need to keep a clear head. Can't get too comfortable at these things." He surveyed the surrounding tables with a jaundiced eye.

Laney chuckled. "Grant it's not an enemy camp. It's just a social event."

"I'll take the guerrilla warfare, thanks."

Laney sipped the iced water at her side. Nine minutes to go.

"How are we doing, folks? Learning great things about each other?"

Laney glanced up at the host beside her table. He waited for an answer and finally Grant supplied one. "Sure. She's a great girl."

The man drifted away, ready to facilitate more meetings, leaving Laney and Grant staring at each other.

"I guess we need to go through with this thing, huh." Grant fidgeted with a stray napkin.

"We could. I know what you do for a living and what kind of car you like. What about hobbies?" Laney smiled.

"I like fishing. Well, not necessarily the fishing part, but the boat and the lake. I like lazing on the water for a day."

"And the beach? Do you like the beach?"

"Sure, sometimes. But not as a steady diet." Grant grinned. "Just enough to make it special, you know?"

Laney nodded. "Uh huh. Kind of like I feel about

snow skiing. I like it but it's not something I want to do all the time."

"You like to ski? What about snowboarding, ever done that?" Grant shifted forward in his seat and leaned his elbows on the table.

"Oh sure. I loved it when I was upright, but once I got down, I couldn't manage to get back up. Looked like a beached fish." Laney demonstrated with hand movements to Grant's enjoyment.

They shared skiing mishaps and segued into other common interests including books and movies. The bell surprised both of them at the end of the session and, after an encouraging wink, Grant moved on.

The event took a break at midpoint, allowing for drinks and stretching. Laney wandered the room, chatting with a few of the other women and a couple of men. Just before recommencing she took a restroom break.

As she washed her hands she talked about the evening with others. Generally, the women in the washroom were divided. Some thought there were possible dates in the mix, others felt it was a waste of time.

"Did you see the tall, muscular guy? The newspaper guy?" A blond reapplied her crimson lipstick as she questioned her friend.

"Did I? He was yummy. And funny. I'm putting his name down for sure." The slightly overweight brunette giggled.

"Honey, I have a feeling every woman in the room

will be writing his name down. He's too good to pass up." The blond twisted around to observe her outfit from another angle. Laney compared their reflections. Her casual skirt and blouse might work for a casual date or a day at the office but up against the skintight pants and low cut blouse the blond wore, she resembled a Sunday School teacher more than an attractive woman on the prowl. Outdated. Not even close to being someone who could attract a man. Not that she really wanted to attract anyone here tonight, she reassured herself. But as she followed the blond and her friend from the restroom, she searched the room for Grant.

He leaned against the bar, a glass of what looked like soda in his hand, and chatted with a brunette. *Now, that's what I want my figure to be like after the plastic surgery.* Laney grimaced at the spurt of jealousy she couldn't deny. The woman had a figure only good money and a very skilled surgeon could achieve. Her red-tipped, obviously artificial nails raked along Grant's shirt sleeve as she leaned toward him. Worse, he laughed at whatever inane remark she made. Laney frowned. What was he doing, ignoring the fast date assignment. She stewed through the bell announcing the start of the second set and all the way back to her table.

During the bottom half of the evening, she tried to concentrate on her fast dates. However, Grant, now in view on her half of the room, chatted with more ladies and bothered her concentration. A quick scan of the room revealed the brunette's table and Laney kept a close eye on Grant's interaction with the woman when he made his rotation at her table.

He didn't go out of his way to flirt but his lazy smile and tousled chestnut hair pulled in most of the women. And he did have great eyes, intelligent and warm. A sharp wit and interests galore. What more could a girl ask for in a date? And why did it irritate her that the other women found him so attractive? She'd outgrown her infatuation with him from her intern days. Hadn't she?

His looks and easy charm, when he wanted to be charming, were a good thing. He might find someone to convince him love was possible. Maybe she should encourage him to jot down some of the other ladies' names. Yeah, she argued with herself. She was definitely over the crush. But she didn't see anyone tonight that would be right for him. Certainly not the brunette with silicone to spare, or the blond from the bathroom. And the giggly friend? Uh uh.

By the end of the evening, all thirty-eight people had been interviewed. The interest guide went home with most of them, to be filled out and e-mailed or posted. Since they'd driven in together, Laney and Grant walked to his car.

Grant drove in silence for a block or two then spoke in his customary rumble. "Did you find anyone you liked at this one?"

"Huh?"

"At the Fast Date thing. There were more fellows

there than you've seen altogether. Surely someone hit you as suitable or whatever you call it."

Laney frowned at his tone. Condescending, patronizing, all the -ing words she could think of. His voice fairly dripped with it.

"There were nice guys there. Just like there were nice ladies too. Did *you* meet anyone?"

"Doesn't matter. I'm not the one who's trying to hook up with someone."

"Neither am I, not really. But it would do you good to go out, mingle. Take your attention off me for a change." The last sentence Laney muttered under her breath.

"I mingle enough." Grant pulled into a restaurant drive-through and turned toward her. "Want a burger?"

"It's after ten."

"So? All this 'mingling' made me hungry. Come on, I'll spring for it." Grant ordered a burger with everything and a soda then turned toward her.

"No thanks. Nothing."

He finished the order and pulled up to wait. "Trying to keep your girlish figure?"

Laney shrugged. "So I watch what I eat. So does every other person on earth."

Grant paid for the order and received his food before pulling into a parking place. "Don't know why, your figure's fine the way it is. And your looks."

"I don't know. I think maybe there were some

women at the Fast Date event that left my figure in the cold. Are you eating that here?"

"Yeah. Cleo's burgers are way too juicy to drive with. I'd end up wearing it." He bit into his burger without responding to her remark about the women at the event.

"Didn't you think there were some attractive women at the restaurant tonight?"

Grant wiped his mouth with a napkin then glanced at her. "You noticed the women more than the men? Uh oh, definitely not a good night for meeting Mr. Right. Don't worry. Just because you aren't built like some of the women at the thing tonight doesn't mean you aren't attractive. You have a nice figure."

"I wasn't fishing, you know."

Grant paused before taking another bite. "No? Well, the comment still stands."

She didn't know how to respond so she didn't. Instead, she settled farther into her seat and let him finish his burger. She pretended to use the streetlight outside to read the preference list from the Fast Date event. After several minutes, she gave in to the temptation to talk.

"What do you think of the column overall, so far?"

"It's going okay, you know that. Wheaton's satisfied and so is Phipps—"

"No, I mean, is the column going okay as far as detailing the singles' scene in the area?"

"I'm not sure that's its purpose, Laney."

"If not that, then what?"

He shrugged. "I have a feeling the column is meant to be an answer to reality TV. Now, don't get upset, it's not that bad. You don't reveal too much of yourself when you write the columns, just enough to hook the reader and keep them wanting more."

"Great. I don't do relationships well, and now I get to share the misery with the public." *Oh, God. Why did I have to share that?*

Grant chuckled. "I get that impression."

"What?" This was getting better and better, she thought.

"It's just that when you're on your dates, you seem a little tense, ill at ease. Like you don't have the confidence or something."

"It has nothing to do with confidence. I'm going out with a stranger, not on my terms, and being watched by you. It's kind of hard to be free and easy."

"You need to loosen up, that's for sure." Grant reached for his soda. Laney quelled the urge to pour the drink over his head.

"And you think you could show me how to be relaxed with a date?"

"I know I could."

"You're on, big guy." Now where did that come from?

Grant smiled in return, started the car, then backed out of the parking space. "Not on a bet."

"So you're backing out. Figures. I think you're more talk than anything else, Grant."

"Not retreating, just calling a halt to the action for now." His voice darkened to match the night. He crumpled his burger wrapper and stuffed it into the well of the console between them, and pulled onto the main road. Just when Laney figured she had enough to fantasize about he rumbled, "Besides, you're not ready for more than talk right now, Lois."

Laney yawned and stretched. The hour or so she'd been home she'd spent alternately analyzing Grant's last comment for the evening and trying to put it behind her. It was like all the other remarks men made. All for effect, to impress, without substance. Still, it prevented her from finishing her work. It was after eleven and she still hadn't completed filling out her interest list.

"This is worse than studying for exams." She sighed and tossed her pen onto the table. She needed a break, bad.

Back when she and Caroline attended college, the trip to an ice cream shop became a regular thing when finals got to be too much. Ice cream and friendly advice seemed to be more valuable around midnight. With a sigh of relief, Laney pushed away from the table to grab the wall phone.

"Hey, Caro. Listen, are you in bed?"

"Not yet. But in a few minutes. Why?" Music flowed

in the background and Laney figured Caro had been lost in one of her guilty pleasures, romance novels.

"I need a BR break. Interested?"

"BR br . . . if you're talking Baskin Robbins you better not be funning with me, girl."

"I'm serious. Want to?" Laney rummaged through her purse for her car keys.

"Give me ten minutes to get dressed."

The nearest Baskin Robbins was fifteen minutes from closing when they ran in the entrance. After retrieving their order from the half-asleep clerk the friends gathered a handful of napkins and returned to Laney's car.

Ice cream dripped in the humid summer night as they settled into the seats, windows open to the breeze.

"Seems I'm destined to eat in the car tonight." Laney sighed with happiness at the chocomocho and rocky road combo ice cream.

"Explain." Caroline studied her with knowing eyes.

Laney briefly outlined her evening and the frustrating conversation with Grant. By the time she finished, the ice cream was gone and so was her buoyant mood.

"Honey, it sounds like he's just trying to get a rise out of you. Ignore him."

"Easy for you to say. You work in a totally different department and don't have to see him every day."

"My loss. He's gorgeous." Caroline licked the last of her ice cream from her fingers.

"You're right though. I just let him get under my skin."

"So what are you going to do about it?"

"Ignore him."

"I doubt you'll be able to do that for long—"

Laney shot her a glare. "Your suggestion. Anyway, right now, I need to figure out what names, if any, to circle on that Fast Date list."

"Let's go over it then."

Laney sighed and let her head fall back on the headrest. "I have, over and over. I've just managed to confuse myself."

"Okay. Forget the specific names, looks, everything. What do you want from a relationship with a guy? More specifically, what do you want *from* a guy?" Caroline pulled an ink pen from her purse and held it ready over a clean napkin.

"Caro, it's late and we need to get home." Laney wasn't sure she needed to dwell on what she wanted in a man. Not tonight.

"So drive. And talk. I'll take notes."

Seeing her friend wasn't going to let it go and, maybe, just maybe it might help her decide, Laney relented. "Fine. I want a guy that listens to me."

"Got it."

"I want a guy who's interested in being active, but wants to do some quiet things on a date too."

"Right." Caro scribbled and nodded in agreement.

"And I want . . . oh, I guess I want a guy that thinks I'm attractive, and acts like it."

"Definitely."

"That's it." *Short list.*

"So, what you need to do when you get home is, without analyzing anything, go over the list and ask yourself—Did this guy listen? Did he mention that he likes being active and laid back at the same time? And did he seem to find you appealing? For the guys that have all of these, check them off or circle them or whatever. No thoughts, no second guessing."

"I'm not sure—"

"No. You have to send this in the morning. Do it when you get home so you don't have to worry about it."

"All right. Deal."

She dropped her friend off at her apartment then drove on home. Once there, she went through the list, using the criteria she and Caro developed. Surprisingly, a few names popped up. She sent a quick e-mail to the Fast Date site before she could change her mind. While online, she e-mailed herself the next installment for the column.

Have you ever heard of fast dating? It's one of those things that have evolved as a result of the rapid-paced world we live in, I guess. But, is it better than the old fashioned way to meet and date? Imagine meeting eight to ten men in one night and being expected, after spending ten minutes with each man, to say whether you want to pursue a relationship with any of them. And did I mention it bears a frightening resemblance to a job interview? Or rather, eight to ten of them?

Grant yawned and balanced his laptop on his legs as he tried to figure out the angle for the next column.

Was the Fast Date idea a new approach? Not really. He remembered his family talking about church socials and such in small town Georgia. What was the difference, really, except the organization? He grinned. There was the angle.

As a modern educated man, I have a lot of opinions about the world. Tonight I formed yet another. We're missing out with our interstate communities. While we have houses in cohesive units, with common street names, we're missing out on neighborhoods. Our parents and grandparents met at church socials and block parties. Instead, today we have to manufacture meeting places and events. Tonight I participated in what fifty years ago could easily have been a tea or community social. But this time there wasn't anyone to introduce me to his cousin.

Chapter Six

"Morgan, you're a flop at this dating business." The city editor glared at her over his glasses.

"I'm sorry, Mr. Wheaton?" Laney stood at the entry to his office. Where was Grant? As co-columnist, he should be in on this, especially if it was going to be a grilling this early in the morning. Had he slept in from the fast dating?

"You've gone out with how many men? Four, five? And not one of them has asked you out for a second time."

"Actually, one did." Laney bit her lip at the slip. Why had she admitted that?

Wheaton perked up. "And you said yes, right?"

"Actually, I told him I'd call him back."

"So do it. Set a date. We need another angle to the

column." Wheaton turned his attention to the stack of papers on his desk, dismissing her.

"But you said it was going well, sir." *Please don't make me do this.*

"And we're going to keep it that way. Do it. Call this man or pick another one of the guys you've seen. Didn't you meet a whole slew of them last night?"

"Yes sir, but I haven't heard back yet." *And I won't make a fool of myself without cause.* Where was Grant?

"You have your assignment, Morgan. Talk to me when you've made a second date." He actually wheeled his chair around and presented his back to her. Well that was definitely a dismissal.

Laney returned to the newsroom and went in search of Grant. What was she going to do now? No man had struck her fancy, not even Craig, the matchmaking guy. And if she had to suffer through a second date, then Grant had to have a root canal or something equal to the pain.

"You look like you've lost your new puppy. What's up?" Grant rounded the corner with a bag of pretzels in his hand. He ripped it open and extended it toward Laney, who gratefully accepted the snack.

"Thanks. You got a minute?"

"Sure. Let's use my desk. That thing you call office space is too tight for me." He ushered her to his area and dropped down into his chair, indicating she should sit in the smaller seat to his right. "Okay, shoot."

"Wheaton wants me to date one of the guys I've met

more than once." She offered the pretzels to him and at his nod, poured some into his hand.

"He does?"

"Yeah, and I don't think I want to pursue anything with any of these guys."

Grant tilted his chair back and clasped his hands in front of him. He studied them for a minute before returning his gaze to Laney.

"You don't want to date any of them?"

"No." Laney crumpled the cellophane package.

"Is it because you were forced to do the column and you've met them through the job?" His posture seemed relaxed but there was something tense, almost fierce in his steady gaze.

She shook her head. "Forced? I chose to do it, Grant. You were the one that was coerced into the thing. But no, that's not the reason. I just haven't connected with anyone I've met, you know? Even Craig, the nice guy from the matchmaking service. He's nice, but just"— Laney shrugged—"nice."

"It's just a date, Lois. Not a commitment," Grant quietly asserted.

"I still have to have a connection. Otherwise it's as if I'm lying to the guy, you know?"

"No. I guess I don't know. That you want to connect with someone is okay, though."

Laney looked at him in surprise. "A compliment, Stone?"

Grant grinned. "Don't let it go to your head."

"So do I call Craig?" She reverted to her problem.

"It was an order. Just like all of the other dates have been, Laney. It's your assignment. And you've said yourself, it won't mean anything, go anywhere."

"Even if I don't like it?"

"You'll get more assignments you don't like than the ones you really crave. That's the breaks when you're a good reporter."

"Two in a row. I'm shocked." He spent so much time getting on her nerves, to be given a couple of compliments in as many minutes unsettled her, even as it sent a warm thrill through her.

Grant picked up his phone and extended it to her. "Call." He stood and retreated. As jittery as Laney was, she needed privacy to call. He filled a cup with water from the cooler and studied his new partner.

Laney tilted her head to the side as she laughed. She really was a pretty thing. Energetic, fun to be around and to needle, and spunky enough to give back everything he dished out. He gulped down the water and refilled his cup.

So, what should a cute girl do? Date a nice, good looking and personable guy. Like Craig. But the very idea of it bothered Grant. Why should it bother him if she dated a guy, any guy?

He gave her five minutes, all the while draining the water cooler and watching her, trying not to dwell on why he wasn't happier things were going his way.

He approached the desk as she replaced the telephone receiver, her expression determined if not pleased.

"He ask you out?"

"Uh huh. We're going out next weekend. To some Italian restaurant he knows on the south side of town."

"Why next weekend?"

Laney didn't make eye contact as she answered, "Oh, you know. His schedule, my schedule—"

"You stalled him, didn't you?" His gut unwound slightly at her reluctance.

"No! I'm busy with research and keeping up with the obits and everything."

Grant chuckled at her blush; she couldn't lie worth a damn. Laney spun around and logged onto the Internet.

"What are you doing?"

"Logging on to see if I have any e-mail, what else?"

"And you're doing it at my desk for what reason?" Grant started sifting through the ever-present file of papers on the side of the desk. Her fresh scent floated to him.

"My e-mail is funky. It closes halfway through the list. I end up having to sign on like four or five times to get everything."

"You need to clean out your hard drive once in a while."

Laney glanced over her shoulder. "I know. I just hate doing it. I'm always afraid something will blow up."

He chuckled at her expression. "I can help you. If

you're still here this evening, I'll stop by and we'll take care of it."

"Thanks, Grant."

Why did she have to look so surprised?

The rest of the day Laney spent thigh-deep in obituaries. By ten that evening, after completing one particularly depressing one, she sighed and signed on to send the file to layout. Or tried to.

"Oh come on! Don't do this to me now." She slapped the desk beside her. Fatigue lessened the thin line of patience she had for her computer.

"What's up?" Grant peered over the cubicle's divider wall.

"This blasted computer. I can't get online long enough to send the file to layout."

Grant entered and leaned over her shoulder to peer at the computer monitor. Her small space tightened even more as he absorbed energy, radiated a strength always present but never acknowledged.

"You want me to help you clean up the hard drive?" His hand hovered over the keyboard.

"Not if you're going to trash my files. I've worked on the obits all day and if you delete them I'll have to do you bodily harm."

"So save the file on a disk and go use my computer to send it. When you're done I'll show you the maintenance procedure."

Laney quickly finished saving the information and slid out from under the computer. She edged past Grant and retreated into the belly of the almost empty news-room. The skeleton evening crew apparently had assignments out of the office.

She signed on at Grant's computer and quickly sent her file to the daily desk. Afterward, she logged into her e-mail.

"Oh help. Not this too," she groaned.

"Laney, are you going to do this or not?" Grant's voice grew stronger as he approached her.

"Not. You need to check your e-mail. We have a mes-sage from the Fast Date event." Laney opened the e-mail and read through the introduction.

"How many guys want to see you again?"

"Let's see, there's a few. John, Carl, Fred, Grant . . ." She looked up at him in surprise. "You indicated an interest in me?"

He nodded slightly. "I tried to be honest, for once."

"And you're interested. In me." Even to her own ears, she sounded baffled.

"Yeah, weird, huh." He moved her to the left and squatted beside her. Quickly, he entered his e-mail account and scrolled down to the Fast Date memo.

"Let's see. Huh. I didn't think that many women went to the thing."

Laney glanced over his shoulder and frowned at the lengthy list of names. "It looks like every woman in the place put your name down."

"Not you." He slanted a look toward her and contin-ued to scroll down. "Wait—"

"I didn't mean—"

"What? That you liked me? Preferred me? Was interested in me?"

"Well, no. Yes. I don't know." She squirmed in her chair at his steady examination. "Here's what happened. I had some trouble coming up with some names and Caro helped."

"Helped? What did she do? Pull names out of a hat?"

"No. She gave me some criteria to use. You know. Just figure out what I want in a man and see if any of the guys . . . met the standard."

Grant stared at her until Laney became uncomfortable enough to stir toward her cubicle. She was halfway there when Grant's hand on her arm stopped her.

"What were the criteria?"

"It doesn't matter," she muttered, her eyes on his shirt.

"Yeah, I think it does." He returned his hand to his side, lightly smoothing it down her arm along the way, as if he couldn't resist.

Laney held her breath, unsure what to do, what to say. Suddenly, this seemed a lot more important than a mere flirtation or a casual date.

"The criteria?" he pressed.

"Um, whether I had things in common with the guys. You know. Like the same type of things."

"Like?"

"Sports, reading, things like that," she hedged. Jeez, why'd she let Caro and the ice cream carry her away?

"Listen, I'll come in a little early in the morning and help you with the cache cleanup, okay? I have some things to check on tonight." Grant moved away and Laney was left with his name on her list, her name on his list, and a whole lot of questions.

"He just left?" Caroline spooned tutti fruiti ice cream with relish as she questioned Laney while they watched a late night talk show from Laney's couch.

"Yeah. We'd just both admitted to being attracted to each other and then he made a lame excuse and walked out of the room."

"He may have been overwhelmed."

Laney snorted. "Overwhelmed? Grant Stone? Fat chance. He's never out of control, never in a situation he doesn't have a handle on. He just didn't want to spend the time on me, on a relationship he doesn't believe in." She fiddled with the remote, trying to adjust the volume. The news program host's tirade on the latest political debacle turned sour the longer he went on.

"Huh?"

Laney stirred the melted ice cream mess in her bowl. All its frozen joys were diminished. Drat. Grant even took that away from her. "We talked about relationships once and he basically said he doesn't believe in true love or anything that involves commitment."

"Totally opposite from your views, in other words."

"Yep."

Caroline finished her ice cream then pushed it away,

along with Laney's bowl. "Well, you're not going to sit here and pity yourself. We need to come up with a plan."

"A plan for what?"

"That's one of the things we're going to figure out. We know you got involved in this thing involuntarily."

"Yeah, but I also decided to take it seriously."

Caro patted her on the shoulder. "And you've had a good attitude even if you don't think any of the men are the one."

Laney growled at her friend. Caro had a way of complimenting and needling you at the same time that left Laney powerless to retaliate. Until later.

Caro continued. "But some things have happened in the process of all this, even though I'm not sure you realized it."

Laney glared. "If you're talking about Grant—"

"I'm not. I'm talking about you. I'm not sure you've seen how many of your insecurities came out. When you had to talk to all those guys, choose them on the Internet, from the personals, and all that, all your bravado disappeared, got tamped down by the fears you had."

"That's crazy."

"No, it isn't. But the other thing that's changed is, after all the stuff you've had to do, you've become more confident. I didn't think there would be any way you'd end up doing all these events, let alone get to the point that you know exactly who you are and who you need in your life.

"So, what we need to decide right now is what do you want to do with the rest of this assignment? Do you want to use it to find a guy to date like you said?" Caro's heartfelt attitude, so often flippant and sarcastic, touched Laney.

Seeing her friend was serious and made a good point, Laney deliberated on the idea of encouraging any of the men she had met. Did she want to date any of them?

"I don't think I feel a connection with any of them."

"None of them? Not a one?"

"Grant. I connect with Grant."

Caro grinned. "Good. So we focus on Grant. Now we need to devise a plan. Do we go heavy or light?"

"Heavy? Light? I'm lost, and still not convinced this is a good idea."

"I'm going to ignore that last part. Heavy is coming on strong, making the first move."

Laney raised a hand to stall her friend. "Not my style."

"Right. Light is more your deal. You continue on with Grant being whatever it is he's been for you."

"Irritating, bossy, exasperating . . ."

"Yeah, like I said. But, as you go on with the same old same old, you add a little something extra. Like flirting with him on occasion, or wearing a different, more elusive perfume. Throw him off balance, make him look twice."

"That is so not my style."

"Make it your style. Either that, the heavy way, or risk having nothing with him."

Laney quietly gathered up their ice cream bowls and headed to the kitchen. She hovered in front of the dishwasher, then shook her head, and veered off to the refrigerator.

"If I'm going to do this, I need something with more power than tutti fruiti. I need rocky road."

Caroline giggled. "Make it two. We have some planning to do."

Chapter Seven

Grant arrived at the office early the next morning. He planned to fulfill his promise to clear out the bugs from Laney's computer but intended to do it when she wasn't in the tiny closet she called office space. Being that close sent his thoughts in different directions.

He booted up the computer and saved her documents to disk before starting the clean up. As he waited for the files to transfer Grant propped an elbow on the desk and rubbed his hand across his face.

His eyes were gritty from lost sleep. The night before he'd rehashed the reasons for writing Laney's name on that blasted list. For a smart man, he reflected, he showed remarkable density in opening himself up like that.

He went through the steps to scan and clean then

kicked back in the chair, almost toppling when he leaned back too far. Laney's chair creaked under the pressure and he surveyed the contents of her workspace.

Her desk looked like an Army surplus item. Though she attempted to lighten the gray metal with plastic figurines and family photos, it still cast a pall on the area. Along with a metal filing cabinet and cubicle dividers, all in boring beige, the overall atmosphere of the cubicle was blah.

He picked up one of the photos, framed in a funky plastic frame. Laney laughed at the camera in a candid outdoor photo, her hair ruffled by a breeze. A taller, male version of her lounged beside her, his arm draped over her shoulder. Her brother? A sense of surprise ran through Grant when he realized he knew little about Laney's family. But from the picture, it looked as if she had a close relationship with at least one member of the clan.

Grant smiled at the picture. Her beauty, he decided, was in her eyes, in her energy. Everything she did, she did with her whole being, every atom. Would she love someone that way? With her whole heart? For life? And if he was the focus of that affection, would he deserve it? A sense of shock ran through him at the thought, the mere contemplation.

Alarmed at the flow of his thoughts, he replaced the photo and completed his task, quickly jotting a note to the effect to Laney. He needed to get to work, and to get to work finding another job.

Later that day, a call to Henry Mills in Chicago further muddied the waters with Delaney Morgan. He chatted with his old workmate for a few minutes and covered his social requirements of asking about wife and family. Then he got to business.

"Hank, what's going on with the city beat position?"

"We're still getting résumés. Can't believe how many there are."

"Good ones?" How much competition would he have?

"Some, fewer than the editor would like to see. None with as much experience as you."

"Do you have any idea when the interviews will begin?"

"The editor plans to call candidates from the phone interviews in a week or so. Expect to hear from him, Grant. I've put in a good word."

"Thanks, Hank. Give Grace my best." When Grant ended the call he refused to dwell on the lack of excitement the news elicited. The position in Chicago, in his grasp, would bring excitement, challenge and, possibly notoriety. He'd be out from under a supervisor who was afraid of him, of assignments that didn't further his career. Be rid of the job of being a voyeur for a woman he'd rather not watch date other guys.

"Hey, Grant. Anyone in there?"

He swiveled around and met Laney's gaze. "Hey, Laney. Got all your death notices etched out?"

"Yep. And I need a break. Want to go scouting with me?" She grinned engagingly.

"Scouting? Where?"

"I need to find a bar."

"A what?"

"A bar. That's next on the list. We need to find one that's good for picking up men." She wheeled around and returned to her workspace to retrieve her purse. As she passed his desk she cast a teasing glance at Grant. "Coming?"

He didn't answer but followed, intrigued by the task ahead, but more by her smile and sassy walk. Something was up and he didn't want to miss it.

His refusal to squeeze into her compact made him the designated driver. After hitting four of the worst dives in the city, they agreed on The Flannel Stop and a time for the planned pickup that evening.

Laney tried to quell the tremors that ran through her body as she fidgeted with her dress. It looked way too tight for the evening, too short, and too coy for her style. And the heels, yikes. If she made it through the evening without a sprained ankle, she'd be lucky.

"Why'd I let Caro talk me into this? I look ridiculous."

She glanced at her watch. No time to change. She had to meet Grant at the bar and stick her neck out, among other things, and try to pick up a date. This, without a doubt, was the worst part of the The Single Life assignment, and that said something.

The drive to the bar should have taken at least forty minutes. Instead she made it in half that time. Who knew Atlanta traffic could be light this early in the evening? The place was dark as she entered and she experienced a moment of panic. Where was Grant? The only reason she had enough gumption to do this was that he would be her buffer.

The country western bar, dimly lit and smoke-filled, even with the ban, hid a multitude of sins. And fostered more. Laney scanned the room for an empty table. She sighted one and scurried to it as fast as her three-inch heels could totter. Once there, she settled into a seat, her back against the wall. *Talk about assuming a battle posture.*

She gave her order for a glass of wine to a waitress then scanned the room. Since she'd been abandoned by Stone, she would have to do this herself. So, first scope out the guys and then narrow down the single and desirable ones, if any existed.

She surveyed her surroundings, taking in the posters of country singers she presumed had sung there, or at least were featured on the jukebox, bumping out tunes at an ear-splitting volume. The brightest lighting in the place, neon beer and wine signs, cast everything in tones of blue and red, making the whole scene something out of a late night film.

A tall man sat in a darkened corner at a table to her left. Dark hair, tall and muscular, his features were cast in shadow but held possibility.

Where was Grant? Giving up on the shadow, she scanned the rest of the room.

The bar was occupied by a cowboy, several suits, a construction guy or two, the ubiquitous college students, along with a few older, noncompetitors. Not a huge pool to choose from, but something to start with.

A movement in the periphery caught her attention and Laney turned. The man at the shadowy table leaned forward to retrieve his drink. Chestnut-brown hair and eyes, highlighted by a candle in the center of the table, coalesced into Grant Stone.

He looked different in this setting; mysterious, almost menacing. Except to her. The earlier feelings of insecurity disappeared, replaced by a more disconcerting feeling. Now, secure in the knowledge he was here and watching, Laney was certain every move she made would be safe with a buffer, but judged by him as well.

She sighed and sipped her white wine. For courage, she remembered Caro's advice. "No matter what you do, never let them see your fear or you're dead in the water." Remarkable how similar dating was to guerrilla warfare.

"Can I buy you a drink, darlin'?" The voice, low and hoarse, preceded the construction guy's approach. Laney glanced up and into sky-blue eyes and started to shake her head. But, no. That wasn't her assignment. So, instead of an icy putdown, she smiled in her best Mona Lisa imitation.

"I'd like that." Jeez, where did the deep southern accent come from? Obviously, years of practice rounding out her i's and shortening her words fled under stress.

"White wine, comin' right up then." He waved a hand for a waitress then returned his attention to her. "Can I sit?"

"Of course." Man, she hated the bar scene.

"Name's Jamie." He leaned forward and propped his bent elbows on the table, his hands clasped in front of him. Laney surreptitiously checked for a wedding band or the telltale line. Nope, no ring. Only strong, square hands with blunt-tipped fingers. Laney lifted her gaze and found him studying her with equal intent.

"I'm Laney. Pleased to meet you." She let her smile broaden slightly.

"Haven't seen you here before. You new in town?"

"No. Do you come here often?" She took a minute sip of her wine. As Grant said a few evenings ago, need to keep a clear head in times like these.

"Couple times a week." His grin was a bit off. "Better than sittin' at home, you know?"

"Mmm." Let it be an agreement or negation; he could decide.

"What do you do for a living?"

Laney skimmed over her job and turned the conversation back to him. Jamie turned out to be very funny. In minutes, he had her laughing and relaxed. While her awareness of Grant and his scrutiny lessened, it remained on the edge of her thoughts.

As the evening progressed Grant finished his beer and switched to coffee. He needed caffeine more than alcohol, at the rate Ms. Morgan was going. He frowned at the sight at her table.

Laney laughed and chatted with Construction guy. And Cowboy, Business Suits and a couple of guys too young to be in a bar let alone drinking, crowded in at her and nearby tables. To a man, the entire bar reacted to her energy, her good looks and smile. What had happened to bring out the flirt?

Grant stood, intent on refreshing his coffee, and on the way to the bar he passed her table. As he edged around the crowd, he caught a sound. More laughter, coupled with a teasing remark focused on Dark Blue Suit. Nothing too forward, just light and playful. And the men, all of them, lapped it up.

He abandoned the coffee and returned to his seat. What did she think she was doing? Didn't she realize what she could start in a place like this? And was she willing to face the consequences?

An hour passed and still males crowded her table. Though the bodies clustered around her changed as men left the bar and others arrived, Laney remained the focus of their attention. The other women in the building couldn't compete and sat morosely on the sidelines.

She didn't flirt overtly. She didn't show a lot of skin or come on to the men clustered around her. Yet, they hovered around her like bees around a hive. And she was the queen bee. She didn't try to single out a guy or better yet, get rid of the whole crew.

His patience at an end, Grant contemplated his

options. How to help extract her from being the princess at the prom? When she rose and, after fifteen minutes of cajoling from her beaus, exited, Grant lingered only long enough to ensure no one followed. Nope, the three women ignored earlier suddenly became belles of the ball.

On his drive home he made a side trip to Laney's apartment complex. Just to make sure everything was secure then head home, he assured himself. Check for her car in the parking lot. Or maybe look to see if the lights were on. He could call and see if she was okay. Then again, knocking on the door would be the best of all. Maybe stay for coffee—

In the end, he checked her car and called her. She assured him she was safe, and added, alone. Then he drove, faster and faster, home.

Laney had mixed emotions the next morning. Her latest adventure at the bar evoked pride in her womanly accomplishments and embarrassment. Did she go overboard? She tried to put her thoughts into words through her column.

Flirting is a dangerous thing. Exhilarating, but dangerous. When I learned to flirt in middle school I realized I had some sort of weird power over boys. I could smile and giggle, bait them with jokes or comments about their favorite sport team, and ensure they wouldn't forget me and may

*indeed ask me to a dance or party. This week I
learned that flirting hasn't changed much. As I
partied and parlayed with grownup little boys
about their hobbies and toys I experienced the
same feelings of exhilaration, fear and foreboding.
Funny how time doesn't change much.*

Grant went into the office late that morning. He
paced the length of his living room, on his third cup of
coffee. It didn't taste like the stuff Laney made him try,
but it provided a much needed kick of caffeine. After
making one more circuit he sat before his laptop and
hammered out the column.

*As the designated voyeur in this series, I've been
privy to several things about the psyche of a
woman. It's fragile. One moment you think she's
invincible, the next, she's shattered by a rebuff.
Women also like to talk about things, a lot. Dress,
manners, and especially men's lack of manners.
The more they can rehash everything, the better
they like it. And last night, I learned the power of
a woman. Seeing a pretty girl smile and innocent-
ly tease a man or several men brought home the
awesome power of a giggle, a twinkle in her eye,
and soft talk. And it strikes fear in my soul that a
woman could have that power over me.*

Chapter Eight

Grant looked for Laney when he arrived in the news-room mid-morning, which worried him. Though he tried to avoid it, he'd gone over the bar scene in his mind, rehashing it too many times.

Still, he couldn't steer clear of the image of her flirting, teasing, smiling at all the other men.

"Hiya, Grant. Ready for a new day?" She breezed up on a scent of caramel latte and floral perfume. She paused at his desk and set a paper cup in front of him.

"What's this?"

"You drink too much of that sludge that passes for coffee in this office. I thought I'd give you another flavor to try."

"I drink that new stuff you suggested at the coffee shop." He opened the lidded cup and sniffed cautiously.

"Yeah, but even then, you order it black."

"I like my coffee plain, so sue me," he grumbled.

Laney leaned toward him to tap the rim of the coffee cup. "Like I said, Grant. You liked the Sumatran blend, you'll like this. You're stuck in a rut. Expand your horizons."

Her smile altered slightly from the original sweet, light one to a more focused curve. *Uh oh.*

"Do you have time to review last night?" He warily sipped the coffee. Not bad.

"Sure. Let me get rid of my purse and I'll be right back."

"No, I'll go with you to your desk." He followed her to her area, his eyes focused on her back. Hell, even her back was cute, covered in a white cotton blouse. Man, was he in trouble.

They settled in the cubicle and silence filtered in. Laney rummaged in her purse for the reporter's notepad she'd scribbled her thoughts on last night.

She grinned as she read the untidy scrawl. She had flirted before, but never with the results at the bar.

"Well, last night was fun, huh?"

"You think so?" He eyed her over the rim of his coffee cup. He slouched in his chair, his eyes boring into her.

She looked at Grant in surprise. "Didn't you have a good time?"

"Not really. I spent most of my time keeping an eye open so nothing happened to you."

"Happen to me? What would have happened? I was in a public bar with a crowd of people all around me. All the rules you keep going over in the column, I followed." Laney turned from him and tapped keys on her computer, bringing the monitor screen to life.

"Do you have any idea of the danger you were in?" His voice cut through her attempt to keep things light. "You had at least half a dozen men hanging around you last night. With the combination of testosterone and alcohol, anything could have happened. And you were lucky it didn't."

"I had everything under control Grant, and you know it." Laney was determined to hold her temper.

"So under control that you left the bar with six guys watching? Waiting to follow you home? Maybe get you alone, where there *wasn't* a crowd, *wasn't* a public place, *didn't* have me around to intercede if necessary?"

She rose and took the two steps to reach her bookcase and the extra box of computer disks. "Well, I wasn't followed. And you didn't have to check on me, either. I'm a grown woman."

"You didn't act like it at the bar," he accused, and stood to face her.

"What's that supposed to mean?"

"You acted more like a teenager at the high school prom than a woman who has any sense."

"Then why were you so bent out of shape by the men who thought I was an attractive *woman*? A woman worthy of spending time with." She wheeled on her heels and left the cubicle. By the time she got to the hallway outside the newsroom, her temper had leveled out a bit.

She huffed a sigh and pushed the down button of the elevator. Right now, with her ego sufficiently deflated by the one man who could do it in a heartbeat, she needed time away from both him and the office. She'd run errands then call and meet Caro for lunch.

Grant cursed under his breath as he rumbled down the aisle of the newsroom. What the hell possessed him to lose his temper, in front of her? She was right, she'd handled herself fine with those guys. Better than fine, she'd controlled a potentially volatile situation with such a lighthearted grace the men probably thanked her for spending time with them before she split!

Grant paused in front of his desk then leaned over and began to gather up some papers. The only thing worse than the way he talked to Laney, he supposed, was the impression he gave her. That he cared. That he was jealous. That wasn't possible. He'd have to care for her in a way he wasn't ready to admit.

He straightened, his briefcase in his hand. "What have I gotten myself into?" He stomped toward the elevator, pausing only to bark at one of the reporters near him. "I'll be at my place for a couple of hours."

Laney persuaded Caro to meet her at the small green space alongside the office building. While it wasn't a park, not much over a parking space, it was private, and that's what the duo needed. They grabbed a bench near the back of the lawn and began their lunches. Caro sipped her soda and nibbled a salad while Laney devoured a sub sandwich.

"Nervous, huh?" Caroline eyed the dimensions of the sandwich warily.

"Hmph?" Laney glanced up in question.

"You only eat that fast when you're worried or anxious."

Laney stalled for time by taking a drink from her soda then wiping her hands. "I'm not nervous, I'm mad."

"At who?"

"Who else? Grant Stone, reporter exasperating."

"What'd he do now?" Caroline automatically went for her cigarettes, realized the pocket in her purse was empty, and grabbed a mint instead.

"This morning, I brought him a coffee, was light and breezy. Instead of thanking me for the coffee, he made faces, put me down for flirting, which I was supposed to do, I might add, on the assignment last night and said I—"

Caro waved her hand to stall Laney. "Take a breath. Take a breath. I understood the coffee, the light and breezy. But what happened with the flirting deal?"

Laney forced herself to slow down. "We had the bar assignment last night. I showed up and kept everything light, not too serious, nothing intense. And it worked, Caro. It worked wonderfully. I didn't play the men, you know? I was nice, pleasant and talkative, not teasing or anything."

"Good, you've always been a girl men like to talk to."

"Right. Well, several of the men asked me for my number, and when I didn't give it to them, they actually gave me theirs. By the end of the evening, I left the bar, went home, and jotted down some ideas for the column.

"Then, this morning, I wanted to try, you know. Try out what we talked about with Grant. Being flirty, intrigue him, get him to see me in a different light. But it backfired like crazy." Laney stuffed the remains of her lunch in the bag, her appetite gone.

"Are you sure?" Caro smiled slightly.

"Positive. He went out of his way to insult me, accuse me of being a tease—"

"Of acting like a man who's jealous?" Caroline snapped open the container of sugar-free mints that'd become her new addiction and popped another in her mouth.

Was it possible? Were the actions, the taunts, and jokes Grant threw at her on a constant basis the result of jealousy? Of seeing her with other guys?

For the rest of their lunch Laney tried to sort it all out. Did she want to entice Grant? And if she did could she deal with the consequences? What did she want from him? A continuation of the column? A relationship? In her three years at the newspaper, she'd never seen him with anyone or date anyone. His social life seemed as doomed as hers, destined to end in first dates. But the funny thing was, she had more fun taking a drive in the country with him than anything she'd done recently. Oh, great. Maybe she was falling for the guy.

That afternoon, Laney worked on her column. A byline, in and of itself, was great, but having to jive the his and hers columns was more than a hassle, especially when she had to rehash the previous evening with Grant. When he refused to speak civilly to her. She settled for reviewing her part of the column to discuss later.

After she went through her e-mail Laney turned to her phone messages. More and more, she was getting the recognition she wanted as a reporter. "And I'll be the next Dear Abby," she grumbled. Not exactly current events or breaking news, but a start.

"Morgan, Wheaton needs us in his office." Grant eyed her warily.

I'm not going to jump you, Grant. Though she might have been tempted earlier, but for reasons other than attraction. He got on her last nerve sometimes. Especially when he called her by her last name.

She gathered her paperwork and trailed her partner, resisting the urge to stick her tongue out at him. Then, tired of following, she hurried the couple of steps it took to come up even with him.

"Scared of me, Clark?"

He glanced at her from the corner of his eye though he didn't slow in his walk to the editor's office. "Don't know what you're talking about."

"Yeah, right. The way you're looking at me, you'd think I was going to sabotage the next Braves game."

His expression turned from guarded to comic as he became aware of her perusal. "Not scared, Lois, just afraid you might be hiding some kryptonite in your bag."

"Meaning?"

"Meaning when women like you start feeling your power over men you become dangerous."

"What power? And I've never been 'dangerous' before."

"Yeah you have; it just wasn't aimed at me." He opened the editor's door, indicating she precede him.

"And you think it is now?" What was she thinking, trying to flirt with him?

"It isn't?" He held her gaze, his expression steady and serious.

"Maybe you haven't seen the full effect," she taunted.

"Heaven help me," he mumbled as she passed him and entered the office.

They sat in the same chairs as usual in Wheaton's office, but Laney had totally different feelings about working with Grant than she'd had at the beginning. Now the assignment didn't seem like torture, but more of a chore that had to be finished in order to get the reward. Maybe this flirting thing could work. And the reward? It didn't seem like a byline was as important as before.

Wheaton grinned at them. "You two have a hit on your hands."

Laney smiled politely. "Thanks."

"We've received more e-mails and letters about The Single Life than any column we started in the past five years." Wheaton waved a sheaf of papers. "And our demographics show that a cross section of the readership want more."

"More?" Laney shot a side glance at Grant. Why did he sit there like a log? "What more could they want?"

"More of a relationship. More dating. More interplay between you two."

"Break it down a little more," Grant gruffly demanded.

With a curt nod Wheaton explained. "Fine. Morgan, you need to start dating someone more than once. The readers want to see a relationship, not just first dates. And Grant, you need to bump up the columns. Giving warnings about safety on dates and waxing poetic about the good ol' days isn't enough. The readership wants more cutting edge stuff."

"Like how it feels to be a voyeur on dates?"

Wheaton ignored the jab. "Finally, the polls indicate there's not enough interaction between the two of you. The inference is that you could be writing columns from two different cities for all the connections that exist."

"So what are we supposed to do? Double date?" Grant stood and stalked out of the room.

Laney hastily excused herself and followed him. "What's wrong with you? Are you *trying* to get us kicked off this assignment?"

Grant ignored her and concentrated on the contents of his desk. She drew closer and bent over the desk, practically in his face. "Talk to me, darn it!"

"Talk to you? You don't want to hear what I have to say, Laney."

"Try me."

He leaned toward her, their noses almost touching. "I'm tired of following your every move. I'm fed up with watching you flirt with men, and hoping you won't do anything stupid. I don't want to continue the column."

Grant's expression mirrored hers, one of surprise and disappointment, as if he hadn't known about his outburst until it came from his mouth.

After a tense, silent moment she faced him off. "How can we not do the column? It's what we've been working for these past few weeks. More recognition, a byline, more readership."

"The column that neither one of us wanted, Laney. Remember?" He stood and walked toward the end of the room.

"Grant, stop! Please."

He halted, his back to her. Then, still not looking at her he said, "If you want to continue the discussion, it's going to be out of here. I've got to get some air."

She rushed behind him, her heart beating so fast she was sure she'd pass out before leaving the building. Instead, she made it to the parking lot and his car. They sped down the street and onto the interstate.

Laney kept her silence as he turned off the exit toward a suburb, her pulse returning to normal. How could he contemplate giving up the column? She hadn't wanted the assignment either, it wasn't her vision of a newspaper career, but neither was writing obits forever. What went through his mind, to throw away the last weeks' work?

When he pulled over beside a small café, Grant heaved a breath. What was he thinking? Running away from a problem, or rather running *with* the problem.

He exited the car and walked to her door, opening it. "I need something to drink. You?"

"I guess," she murmured, and smoothed a dark curl behind her ear.

She's nervous. The thought surprised him. Laney had shown lots of emotion since working with him, chiefly anger and frustration, but never anxiety. It had to be due to his pulling out of the column. Well, he'd talk her into it. He had to. He had to be ready when something came through in Chicago or New York. Things were getting too close here.

They settled in a small booth and Laney grabbed the plastic-covered menu then hid behind it.

"They don't offer much other than sandwiches and fries here," Grant said.

"Sometimes, that's exactly what you need. That and a milkshake."

"Yeah, comfort food." He glanced up as a waitress approached them.

They placed their orders and waited for the requisite water and napkins to arrive. Laney sipped hers while he idled. Soon, after she gathered her thoughts, she would start her arguments.

She didn't disappoint. "Grant, you've got to continue the column."

"Why?"

For a moment she looked at a loss. "Why? Well, because it is helping both of our careers—"

"How? By making you the Dear Abby of the Gen Y set? And making it even harder for me to get a job covering crime or the world news beat? A byline isn't always a good thing, Laney."

She leaned forward. "If we make a stupid idea into something quality, it is. And that's what we've been doing. Even the naysayers, you and me in particular, have to acknowledge the column is giving some good advice."

"Advice not to go out on dates with losers?" He tried for a joke and got a small smile in return before she reprimanded him.

"The guys, by and large, are pretty nice, just shy or a little clueless about how to approach a woman."

"Yeah." He didn't want to continue this thread of conversation. "Look. You wanted to be taken seriously. Continuing with this column isn't the way to do it."

"And leaving a job half finished isn't going to do your reputation any good, either. You wouldn't get another decent assignment with the paper and you know it."

His silence told her more than he wanted. Her face paled slightly, highlighting the few freckles sprinkled across the bridge of her nose. "You're thinking about leaving the paper, aren't you?"

"Probably. It's time."

"Time to go? Is it the column? Because I said yes and you were pressured into it?" She ignored the sandwich and fries the waitress placed in front of her.

Grant leaned back to allow his order to be placed on the table, and held her gaze. "It wasn't the column, and you were pressured into it just the same as I was. I haven't had a future with the paper since Wheaton and I were up for the same position."

"But you've been able to work with him since he got the job, right?"

"In a sense, but I'll never make it beyond the occasional local news story and human interest stuff, like the column."

"With your experience? That's not good use of your talents."

Grant sent her a look. "Yeah."

"Why would Wheaton be so mean?"

"Because he was second choice for the job, Laney."

"You turned down the editor position?" City editor at his age, it was a great opportunity. "Why?"

"Because I didn't want to leave the field yet." Grant shook his head. "Maybe I should have. I didn't think of the ramifications of turning the job down, or of the possibility that Wheaton would find out about it. I should have, I just didn't want to acknowledge that I might not be able to work with him anymore." He gestured toward the food. "Eat."

Laney glanced at the burger and fries in front of her. When they arrived she'd been nervous enough to eat everything on the menu. Now, nothing tempted her. She returned her gaze to Grant. "When are you leaving?"

"I don't have a job yet, just some nibbles."

"But you know a lot of people and you've got great credentials. You'll get something soon." She finished, miserable.

"I'll probably be gone by the end of the year."

"Right. Does anyone else at the paper know?"

"No, and don't spread it around okay?"

"Yeah, sure." What else was there to say? Except that she didn't want him to go, she wanted him to stay and be with her. Argue with her, give her the energy to meet strangers, even silly men who didn't fill her with the giddiness he did when he smiled.

Oh, Lord. She loved him and she was sunk.

A French fry drenched in ketchup appeared in front of her. Laney lifted her gaze from her plate, and met his gaze. Uncharacteristically gentle, his eyes smiled as he waved the fry in front of her. "Eat, Lois. We need to hash this out and you need your strength."

She bit the fry, the tangy ketchup clashing with the warm crispness of the home fried potato. As she chewed he took a healthy bite from his sandwich. He wasn't going to be gone for a few months. For that time, she decided, she wanted to work with him, be beside him as much as possible. And maybe, just maybe, get him out of her system. Surely, he'd make her angry and ticked off just enough she'd want to be rid of him, right?

She gathered her burger in her hands and lifted it to her mouth. Just before biting into it she made her decision. "Before we leave this place, Grant Stone, I'm going to have your word."

He shot her a suspicious look. "My word on what?"

"Your word that we see this thing to the end. That we work on the column until the initial assignment is over. And that, when you leave, you leave with a clean slate."

Chapter Nine

Grant cursed under his breath as he entered the darkened movie theater. A traffic snarl on the expressway put him behind, and now he had no idea where Laney and her date sat.

He snarled an apology and stepped over the legs of a couple totally uninterested in the previews. Probably wouldn't be watching the main attraction either, from their actions. He exited the other end of the row of seats. God knows he didn't need a reminder of couples and making out in movie theaters.

In the days after their trip to the diner, Laney remained largely noncommunicative. She answered questions with short, simple sentences. Then, yesterday afternoon she informed him she had a follow-up date with Craig, her matchmaker date. The one guy she connected with.

He finally gave up on his search for her in the darkened room and sat on an aisle seat, faced with the prospect of sitting through a romantic comedy. Who picked the movie? If Laney, she was looking for a relationship for sure. No man worth his salt voluntarily watched a cute blond frolic around town looking for true love when he could enjoy a car chase or three.

Or worse, what if Craig chose the movie? That meant he was serious about making an impact on her. Make her think he was sensitive and all that crap. Next, he'd be taking her to a darkened restaurant with frilly tablecloths and candles.

The feature started and Grant ran a hand over his face. He had become as bad as the hero in the film. Dwelling on his competition when he didn't have any intention of following through with his attraction—

God, he was more than attracted to her. If he didn't love her, no way on earth would he have shown up at this show. No way would he have agreed to finish the column.

A laugh caught him by surprise, a low, throaty giggle and way too familiar. He craned his neck to see in front of him, two rows ahead, the top of a tousled head that barely cleared the headrest. Beside her, not too many inches away, rested a blond head.

A feeling of relief surged through Grant followed

quickly by irritation as the blond head tilted toward hers. What was he doing? Whispering sweet little nothings in her ear? Making promises he couldn't keep? Grant leaned forward, cursing the theater's efficient sound system.

When Laney's date stood and left the theater, Grant took advantage. He slid out of his seat and moved to the seat directly behind Laney.

"Psst."

Dark eyes appeared above the top of the headrest, soon followed by the rest of her head. "Hey. What are you doing back there?"

"What I'm supposed to be doing. Shadowing you."

"You don't shadow me by sneaking up and stalking me." She started to turn back in her seat.

"Yeah, well I'm not enjoying it too much, myself. I'll leave you and Junior alone if you want." Or at least withdraw to a more discreet distance.

"What's going to happen in a movie theater, Grant? We're watching a comedy and sharing popcorn, for cripes sake."

"You clearly haven't been to a movie in a while."

She glared at him and opened her mouth, ready to get them both thrown out of the theater when her gaze shifted behind him. "Craig's coming back. I'll talk to you later."

Grant sank into the seat and crossed his arms over his chest. So she didn't think a movie date could produce anything? Man, would he like to prove her wrong. But not tonight. If surf guy tried anything, he'd find himself wearing the soda he'd just bought.

The movie crept by. Grant tolerated the noise level and gritted his teeth through the kissing scenes. He barely restrained himself from going over the seat, when Craig clasped Laney's waist as they edged out of the row after the film. What did the jerk have planned for later in the evening?

The fancy restaurant featured frilly tablecloths and candles. A live jazz band played discreetly in the background, the only thing Grant found agreeable about the whole evening. Man, Laney's date was trouble. Or would be if he slid any closer to Laney. Grant forced himself to sip his beer instead of gulping it.

His table, situated next to the kitchen, offered the worst possible view of Laney. He had to lean away from the table to see her back. Only her body language told him how the evening progressed. Since he hadn't been able to read her the entire time they had worked together, this didn't look promising either. He only knew when she was nervous by how much food she packed away.

His expense account wasn't going to suffer much in spite of the overpriced menu, since he had no appetite for fois gras or duck l'orange. And he was going to throw his back out with the contortions he had to go through to keep an eye on her.

"Grant Stone, who would guess I'd run into you here?"

A body obstructed his gaze and Grant pulled himself into an upright position before he glanced up. Laney's friend, the one who smoked, stood smiling at him, one hand on her hip.

"Well, are you going to ask me to sit? I've just barely managed to convince the maitre d' we're together." Her smile thinned a bit at his hesitation.

"Go ahead, sit." *What's her name? Karen? No, Carolyn? Not quite, Caroline, yeah that's it.*

"My, how gracious you are. I can't understand why Laney didn't want to work with you." She smiled through her sarcasm. A waiter approached and took her drink order and his request for a refill.

"Laney didn't want to work with me because we had a stupid assignment." Grant shifted his chair a bit so he still had a view of Laney's table, if not of her.

"Well, that too. But she's done well with it, don't you think?"

"Sure. She's a good writer, always has been. Just needed something to sink her teeth into."

"Have you told her that?" Caroline's smile disappeared, leaving an earnest gaze Grant didn't really want to meet.

"Look, Caroline—"

"Caro."

"Right. I'm not sure what's going on, but I'm trying to work here." And no way did he want this right now.

"I know. Laney and her second date with Craig. I just wanted to lend a little"—she paused thoughtfully—"a little moral support. To both of you."

"Support? For what, dinner?"

"Well, the whole thing has gotten a little more serious than you anticipated, hasn't it?"

What did she see? And if Caroline could tell he was attracted to Laney, did that mean Laney saw it too?

"How serious it is, is between Laney and me, don't you think?"

"Is it? If the column is as successful as Laney said the editor implied, it could mean more for both of you. Oh, isn't that what we were talking about?" She arched an eyebrow, all but laughing at what he was sure was a flush. He accepted a second beer and the waiter placed a glass of wine in front of Caroline.

"Yeah. We're working through the resolution of the column. It'll be over within a few months, I'm sure."

"And you'll both go on to bigger and better things. Wonderful." Caroline sipped her wine and winced.

"Something wrong with your drink?"

"No. I just have a sensitive mouth." She pushed the drink away and replaced it with her iced water.

"Dental work?"

"I'm addicted to sugar-free mints, can't stop eating the stuff."

Grant shook his head and gave up the battle of understanding her: Just like Laney, too convoluted for his simple brain.

"Has Laney mentioned her plans for after the column's end?"

Caro shook her head. "Not really. I think she's looking for someone to see regularly but I don't know if any guy has caught her fancy yet. Maybe Craig—"

"What are you talking about? I asked about her job, not her dating life. Besides, all this stuff with dating, it was all just the assignment." Wasn't it? Grant frowned at her.

"Well, sure. It started out that way. But look at her. She's more confident in talking with men, in meeting new people. She's grown up, our little Laney."

"Yeah, grown up." He sometimes wished he had the prickly, insecure Laney from months ago. He wasn't sure how to handle the new, more confident Laney or the feelings she brought out in him.

"As to her job, she's not said much. I'm sure she wants another byline, maybe another column. She's even asked me about writing some for the society page. But whatever it is, if she's out of obits, she'll be happy."

Maybe Laney's friend didn't know her as well as she thought she did, Grant mused. Laney wanted more. More challenge, more stimulating than a column on who wore what where. Something that required her to stretch her writing muscles.

He sat through a boring dinner, trying to make conversation with Caroline, all the while wanting to see Laney up close, to talk to her.

The next morning, he prepared his article for the column, then reread it. It didn't necessarily talk about dating but it had to be said.

Life's strange, how it throws you curves. When a job comes along, you take it because it's the next step in your plans for your life. And when a bump in the road occurs, you stumble over it, brush off any dirt you've gained and move on. But sometimes, you have a bit of time to ponder your decision. Do you move on and take a chance on the new person in your life, or do you play it safe and continue on with your path? Scares the life out of me. What about you?

Laney finished her article for the column in record time that morning. As she saved it to her hard drive she wondered, why had she argued with Grant to keep the column, when she hated every minute she had to spend dating on command?

Second dates. How awkward are they? When I agreed to do the column, I knew I'd be meeting lots of men, or at least several. And first dates are a trial, no matter what, with introductions, awkward pauses, and figuring out how soon to end the date. But second dates lend themselves to more. More discomfort because you've just given the guy a clue that you're interested enough to wear heels. Also, you have to think about how much informa-

tion you should disclose. Do you spill everything? Give him a clue how insecure and scared you really are? Or do you lie through your teeth and try to convince him you are the one person who's remained single this long because you are too perfect for words? What a quandary.

Chapter Ten

"What is this?" Laney threw down the column and dug into the opened bag of cheese puffs for another handful.

"Quit eating those things, you're going to become a blimp." Caro reached toward Laney's coffee table for the bag.

"If you want to keep that hand you'll not do that," Laney shot back, retrieving the bag, and clutching it to her chest with a rustle of orange puffs.

"Laney, honey. Calm down."

"Calm down? Calm down! How can I calm down when my best friend is sabotaging me? How can I calm down when I'm supposed to go out with Craig again, and I don't even want to do more than dive into this bag of cheese puffs?

"Forget that Grant hasn't talked to me in days, beyond making sure I don't make a move on the column without him? Calm down when I can't figure out what the heck he wrote this week's column about?" Her voice ended on a hysterical note and she stuffed her mouth again, more to keep it busy than anything else.

"Look. I didn't sabotage anything when I went to the restaurant. I wanted to see how things were going. And you said yourself Grant seemed kind of weird about you going out with Craig again. And I saw plenty, I have to tell you."

"What do you mean?"

Caroline reached across the sofa and handed Laney a napkin. "Wipe your mouth. I mean he was miserable. And the only reason a man should be miserable in my company is if he wants to be with someone else."

"Really?" Laney mumbled around her snack.

"Really. Although that's been happening more lately." Caroline sipped on her diet soda.

Laney waved her hand dismissively. "Get back to me, Caro. We'll deal with your love life later. How was he miserable?"

"When I was talking about you hooking up with someone you met through the column."

"Hooking up? Why would I want to do that? I haven't met anyone that I like that well." And no man interested her more than Grant.

"You have, but he doesn't know it yet. Remember? And what happened to the plan of flirting with him?"

"I don't know how." Laney stared glumly into her empty bag of cheese puffs. She moistened a fingertip and ran it along the side of the bag to gather remnants of cheese flavor.

"Don't do that!" Caro grabbed the bag from her and crumpled it.

Laney stuck her finger in her mouth and mumbled, "I know. I'm out of control. I ate an entire box of choco-blockos last night."

"All eight of them?" Caro's eyes widened.

"Yep. Eight chocolate snack cakes iced with chocolate icing. And a two liter of diet soda."

"Well, that cancels out like two calories." Caro stood and pointed a finger at Laney. "You have to straighten up, and right now."

"But I'm failing at flirting with Grant. I'm lousy at this meeting-new-men stuff. And the only reason Craig is going out with me on more than one date is he's sure he's going to get a plug for his computer software business in the column."

"You have the self-esteem of a gnat right now. Look, we're going shopping for a few hours. We'll figure out the flirting thing while we shop. Then, when we get back, we'll decipher Grant's column. Now go wash off the orange dust and let's get going."

"Can we go to the grocery?"

"No."

Laney dropped onto her sofa, bags of shoes and skirts rustling around her. "Remind me, the next time I go shopping with you, I'm leaving my wallet, my checkbook, *and* my credit card home."

"You needed the heels for your date tomorrow." Caro opened her bags and started checking her purchases.

"Like you needed another pair of pink shoes?"

"The tan offset the pink in them. And you have to admit"—Caro held a delicate low heeled slipper aloft—"they're beautiful."

"Yeah, but you'll be paying for them for the next four months."

"I've been saving my cigarette money. You'd be surprised what you can buy when you quit smoking."

"No, I wouldn't. And I'm proud of you." Laney smiled as Caro approached the counter dividing her kitchen and living room. She nodded when Caro held an empty glass up and waited while she delivered two soft drinks to them.

"Thanks. Now, at the risk of bringing you back down, did you check your messages?" Caro nodded toward the message machine on the counter.

"No." Laney stood and cautiously approached the phone. It flashed with an annoying light, indicating messages. She pushed a button and pulled a notepad toward her.

"Hey, Laney. Grant. Just wanted to touch base about tomorrow night. What's the plan? Call me."

She paid little attention to the other two messages,

including one from Craig indicating his eagerness to tell her about his new venture. After deleting the messages she turned back to Caroline, her mood pensive.

"What did he mean, Caro?"

"Just that he wants to coordinate his snooping, I guess."

"You know what I'm talking about."

"The column? Let's see." Caroline plucked the paper from the coffee table. She read through the words silently and then glanced toward Laney.

"You tell me. What do you think he meant?"

"If he was talking about dating and all that, then he meant a second date can lead to more, maybe a relationship." But she didn't think he referred to dating, at least not the column's dating scene.

"And if he meant more?" Caro pressed.

Laney sighed. "If he meant more, then I have to decide. Am I going to make an idiot of myself and go for it or am I going to be the chicken I've always been and let it go?"

"And that, my girl, is the biggest decision you have to make. Maybe that's what he ultimately was talking about. Every decision we make affects us for the rest of our lives, and other people. Think about it, Laney. Do you want to spend the rest of your life thinking about what you *didn't* do?"

"Good night, Craig. Thanks for a lovely time." Laney backed away as she spoke, determined to get out of the expected good night kiss. Craig advanced as she withdrew until her back was against the wall of her apartment building. Between her and the door, a scant foot away, stood her date.

"I'm really enjoying our time together, Delaney." He smiled, his teeth all but glowing in the dark.

"Good. Well, night."

"And my friends are all wondering . . ." He leaned and rested his weight on his extended arm, his hand propped against the wall an inch away from Laney's shoulder.

"Wondering?" Could she duck under his arm and make it to the door before him? She eyed him, no. He looked too much like a runner.

"Well, you're writing the column on The Single Life, and you talk about the dates and everything—"

"Yes?" *Here it comes.*

Craig shrugged but his expression resembled a sulky little boy. "Well, you haven't mentioned my name. Haven't mentioned what I do, what I look like, anything."

Haven't given your business a plug. "I don't mention names, Craig. I want to ensure confidentiality."

"Oh, I don't mind—"

"Thanks, but I've seen other men. And they've all been nice when I told them about the column. I can't start using names now, or it would be an indication I'm not true to my word that I'd protect everyone's privacy, now wouldn't it?"

She took a step forward to allow room to access the building entrance. Craig had to step back or lose his balance. "Night, Craig."

She opened the door to her apartment building and slipped inside. Outside, Craig rambled on a moment before grumbling at her then stomped down the walk.

Thank God that was over.

She'd been miserable all evening. Her feet hurt from her new shoes, her jeans were too tight, thanks to the cheese puffs and choco-blockos, and she hadn't been able to spy Grant all evening. Of course, it would have been tough when the whole stadium was on their feet for the baseball game. And her head hurt from the noise.

She leaned against the wall and eased off her shoes. Even climbing public stairs in bare feet was preferable to wearing the pointy toed short boots any longer. In the store, the shoes were irresistible but now, her feet resisted being transformed into genie feet.

The cool and quiet apartment welcomed her with a soft glow from a single lamp she'd left burning at the beginning of the evening. She dropped her boots beside the door and advanced into the room, intent on finding an aspirin and jotting down some notes before turning in.

A flashing light indicated her machine had more messages to deliver. She ignored it and, after swallowing a couple of aspirin, changed into her sleep shirt and flopped onto her sofa with a notepad and pen.

She'd scribbled a couple of lines down when her

purse began to vibrate. With a sigh, she reached inside and found her cell phone and flipped it open.

"Where are you?" Grant's voice grated across the line.

"At home, why?"

"You're home? When'd you get there?"

"About fifteen minutes ago. Where are you?" She tossed the notepad down; any thought of recording her ideas had gone out the window with his voice.

He rumbled into the phone, his voice slightly more relaxed. "I'm driving on the interstate from the stadium. I lost sight of you in the eighth inning. Did the end of the date go well?"

"Well enough. What do you mean you lost sight of me?"

"I had to move a couple of rows up when a fistfight broke out. You and your date must have moved too, 'cause by the time I got settled, you were gone."

"Actually, we left a little early, since we were losing anyway." She grinned at his groan.

"Tell me about it. I stayed to the bitter triple-play end. Next time we go to a ball game remind me to take a book to keep me awake."

"Does that mean you're willing to go to another game with me?" she teased, hopeful.

"Only if we get to sit in the same row next time. Preferably next to each other," he finished with a softer note.

Was he flirting with her? Please let it be so. "It's a

deal. We go to the game, eat hot dogs and peanuts, and yell ourselves hoarse." It sounded like heaven.

"Sounds good to me. Look, I needed to tell you . . ."

His pause felt like hesitation and that wasn't Grant Stone at all.

"What?"

"I'll be out of town for a few days."

"Where are you going?" *And will you come back?*

"Chicago. I have an interview."

"Oh. For a good position?" She tried to infuse some enthusiasm in her voice but it was a pitiful effort.

"Yeah, the city desk. It'll be a nice step up."

And too far away. "Well, good luck, though you don't need it."

"Yeah, well . . . I just wanted to let you know. I'll leave my part of the next column with you before I leave."

"Okay."

"Listen, Laney." For the first time since they started the column, he sounded nervous.

"Yes?"

"After I get back . . . well, I want to take you out."

"Take me out?"

"Yeah, on a date."

"A date." Now? When he may be moving away?

"Yeah. Dressing up, making small talk, just you and me."

"And no third party, huh?"

"No. What do you say?"

"I'd like that."

"Great. Seven o'clock three days from now, okay?"

"Okay. Where'll we be going?"

"I'll give you a call about that. I have to plan something to top a losing baseball game." His voice lost its edge and Laney felt the thrill of flirting that counted for something. Flirting with Grant.

"Okay." She ended the call with a sigh, suddenly aware of the absence of her headache. But the bigger question was, how was she supposed to sleep for three days?

"Hello?" She sounded tired but not sleepy.

"Hey, Laney. It's Grant." He leaned against the headboard of the hotel bed and closed his eyes. The past two days melted away with the sound of her voice.

"How was your flight?"

"Fine. Longer than I would have liked." His shoulders ached from sitting in a coach seat several inches too short for him.

"And your interview?"

"It went okay." He paused, unsure of whether to tell her. "They offered me the job. It's not official but . . ."

The pause that followed almost convinced him his connection had been cut, then Grant heard her clear her throat.

"Congratulations, unofficially."

"It's not written in stone yet. It'll have to go through the executive offices and I may have to come back to Chicago for a follow-up interview, but—"

"But you're probably in."

"Yeah." A job he'd been after for years, for more years than he could remember. A job covering major stories, offering national exposure and the opportunity to move up, and he didn't want it. "Did your date with Craig go okay? You went to the theater, right?"

"Uh huh. It was fine, I'll tell you about it later. Look, I have to go. I've got to finish up my part of the column before deadline." Was there anything in her voice to imply she didn't want him to take the job? That she wanted him to stay?

"Right. Well, talk to you when I get back."

"Okay, 'bye."

Grant closed the cell phone and tossed it on the second bed. He needed to be back in Atlanta, bad. How was he going to make her understand, when he couldn't understand himself? He wanted the job, but he *needed* Atlanta. Or maybe it was Delaney Morgan he needed.

"So, is our date still on?"

Laney struggled to wake. "Grant? What's wrong? We talked a few hours ago." She glanced at the clock. "It's three in the morning."

"Sorry, time change."

"The time isn't that different, Grant." She sat up in bed. "Are you still in Chicago?"

"Nope. I got an earlier flight. I'm over Ohio right now, or maybe Kentucky." His voice sounded downright chipper for this time of the night, or morning, darn him.

"Call me when you get home." She yawned.

"Why? You're awake now."

"But, not happy." She sighed. "Okay, what was your question?"

"Are we still going out when I get back?"

"Yes, but not until the sun comes up."

"Funny. You're funny when you're half asleep." His voice rumbled in her ear, sending warmth through her.

"Yeah, but wait 'til I wake up. Then you'll be sorry."

"So, here's the plan. I'll pick you up at seven tomorrow—"

"You mean tonight."

"Right, tonight. And we'll date."

Laney chuckled at his tone. As if he anticipated awkward silences, and being afraid that you had food in your teeth. "Where are we going?"

"It's a surprise."

"If you don't tell me, you'll be in for a surprise when you expect me to dress up and I show up in jeans."

"Oh, yeah. Well, just dress casually, but cute, like you do at work."

Laney's smile widened. "Okay. Cute casual it is. See you at seven."

"Bye, Lois."

She hung up her phone and eased back under the covers. How was she supposed to sleep now? Now that she knew he thought she was cute? Who knew cute could be a good thing?

She sat back up and retrieved a notepad from her

bedside table and rewrote her column. Sometimes, a simple conversation changed everything.

What is it that makes another person attractive? His hair, physique, his way of walking? Is the whole pheromone, chemical thing to blame? Or, in the end, is it that weird, scary thing we dream of and read about, that thing called kismet? How can you meet someone for the first or fifth time without realizing you don't want to spend your life without him? And what event has to occur for you to realize your life is complete when you are sitting across a table at the café from the one person who understands your moods, who laughs at the same jokes you find funny?

Was she jumping the gun, she wondered? How would Grant react when he read the article? And what did his say?

When affection and caring becomes more, the responsibility that accompanies it is frightening. Suddenly, you become responsible for another's life, another's happiness, even another's future. Are we ready for that responsibility? Do we even want the task of determining another's life when, let's face it, we don't run our lives all that well.

Chapter Eleven

Laney twisted and turned in front of her mirror. Was the dress too short? Too long? Too flowery? She sighed and shrugged her shoulders. Grant had seen her in jeans, casual clothes, and even after a rain shower at work. So what was the big deal?

The deal was she had a *date* with the man. A real, honest to God date. Never mind she didn't know where they were going or what they would do. It was a date, complete with chitchat, and maybe a kiss at the end of the evening.

She scrambled around her living room, picked up her running shoes and a dirty dish, and stowed them. After running a dust cloth along the edge of her coffee table, she smoothed her hands down the skirt of her dress. Fifteen minutes 'til seven.

The dress was a stretch, maybe she should change—

The doorbell pealed and she jumped slightly before heading to open it.

He lounged against the frame of the door, one hand in the back pocket of his jeans, a simple white collared shirt setting off the brown highlights in his hair.

"Hey." He smiled gently at her.

"Hi, come in." Laney opened the door wider. "I didn't know if a dress would be okay for the evening, so—"

"You look great. I like that color on you." His eyes scanned over her and she turned away to hide her blush and grabbed her purse.

"Am I going to like this?"

"You're going to like it. Ready?" He held out a hand and with a sense of change, she grasped it.

"I love this place, how did you find it?" Laney leaned back on one extended arm and sipped her wine as she glanced around the small park.

The blanket, the warm summer night filled with music, the light picnic, everything was just as he'd planned.

"I did a story on the demise of drive-in movies and how businesses are trying to pull in visitors for the sites." Grant scanned the area. Smaller than a city parking lot, the area was filled with couples and families, each with their own blanket or chairs, enjoying the warm summer evening and live jazz.

"The owners have movies here too. They show old forties films on the weekends, along with a concert."

Laney turned a rapt face toward him. "Can we come for that too?" As soon as the words left her mouth she bit her lip and looked guilty.

Grant rushed to assure her. "I'll find out what the next movie is. Is the chicken okay?"

"It's great. Food, music, good wine, and great company. What more could we ask?" Laney smiled at him and sipped again.

Amazing how long a glass of wine could last, Grant noted. She looked relaxed but he could swear she was nervous.

Several couples stood and began to sway to the music. Grant stood and held his hand out to Laney. "Dance with me?"

Her eyes shone as she rose. The music matched the night, warm and sultry. Laney's head came to rest on Grant's shoulder as he pulled her closer into his arms. The dance couldn't last long enough for him.

The evening passed rapidly, too quick for his taste. The jazz band provided an occasional slow number they took advantage of. During the more lively songs, they found more things to talk about. Suddenly, the last set concluded and Grant faced the end of the evening with her.

They drove to Laney's building in near silence, both lost in the mood of the evening. Grant's gaze lingered on Laney, her hair caressing the nape of her neck in soft waves, mussed by the light breeze from the open car windows. She looked sleepy, relaxed. And beautiful.

He cleared his throat. How was he supposed to tell her about tomorrow's column? They hadn't talked about the current issue's installment before deadline, and he had no idea what her column contained. But one thing was sure. Once she read his, she'd know he was falling for her. And he'd rather tell her before she opened the paper over her breakfast bagel and coffee.

"Laney—"

"The evening was great, better than any evening I've been on lately." She turned her head to gaze at him and he smiled in return.

"Even the experimental theater you went to with Craig the other night?"

She groaned, "Oh, help. That was beyond strange. I never thought I'd spend two hours watching people dressed up like facial body parts expounding on the meaning of life. I dreamed a giant nose chased me the next night." She shuddered and frowned at his laughter. "And you had to be in Chicago at that time."

"Well, if it's any consolation, I had to sit through an opera performance with the editor at the paper. Hate that stuff, can't understand a word of it."

She chuckled slightly in acknowledgement of his attempt to recapture the ease of their date, but the mention of Chicago left it strained.

Grant turned off the interstate and onto the street that led to her apartment. *Not much more time,* he thought. *Get to it.*

"I want to tell you something."

"You accepted the position?"

"No, not that. It's about you and me. Us."

Laney twisted around in her seat. "Us?"

"Yeah. The fact that I think there is an us."

"Oh." For once, she didn't have a comeback.

He pulled into the parking lot of her complex and quietly found a parking place in front of her building. He turned off the ignition to a silence more deafening than the roar of the engine and road.

Grant released his seat belt and faced Laney. "I don't know where this is leading. I don't even know if it's going to go anywhere past tonight, but you need to know something before you leave this car."

She arched a brow at him. "Why before I leave the car?"

"Because you'll read the column tomorrow and I want you to know where I'm coming from."

"The column. Well, you might need a preface to mine too."

"Yeah?" He was momentarily distracted by her fidgeting with her seat belt but returned to his task. "I'm . . . oh, hell. I sound like a soap opera star or something, but I'm going to say it. I'm attracted to you. Really attracted."

Laney stared at him a moment before breaking into a chuckle. "I know that, Grant. If I didn't know it before tonight, I would have guessed when you complimented me on my dress."

"I've always thought you were cute."

"Cute, yes, but you never bothered to say anything until recently. And when you did, I figured you finally saw me as something more than an irritant."

"Oh, you still irritate me," he mumbled, and grunted when she socked him in the arm. She immediately smoothed her hand down his shirt sleeve and he caught her hand in his. He wasn't sure but he thought he caught a blush riding along her cheeks, and he squeezed her palm.

"If it's any consolation, my column is about the same thing. Somehow, you've gotten under my skin as well. God help me." This time, when she smiled the curve of her lips were tinged with something he wondered at. Sadness? Desperation?

"What's wrong with being attracted to me? If we're both attracted, and want to spend time together, what's the problem?"

"Nothing, absolutely nothing. Now, I have to go inside. Have a full day tomorrow, you know. Another date to set up with, oh, somebody." She reached her hand out to open the door.

"Hold on, let me." He unfolded his body from the car and rounded the hood to open her door and extend a hand to her. He retained his grasp on her hand as they walked inside her building and up the stairs. At her door, Laney turned and tilted her face toward him with a farewell grin. He leaned down, intent on getting a kiss. Before he could make contact though, she side-stepped and slid inside her apartment.

"'Night, Grant. See you tomorrow."

"Tell me again, why do we like men?" Caroline plopped into the chair beside Laney's desk and stuck her crossed ankles out to the full extent of the floor space.

"Because we like being miserable?" Laney propped her chin on her hand and stared back at her friend. Her eyes were gritty from lack of sleep, and she had to force herself not to watch for Grant all morning.

"I know why I'm unhappy. Why are you?"

"You first. What happened with the doctor?" Laney pulled open her middle desk drawer and withdrew the last of her shortbread cookie stash. As she offered Caro one she scribbled a note to replenish her snack drawer.

"Found out he wasn't really a doctor. Doesn't even play one on TV." Caro munched a cookie, making it last far too long, in Laney's opinion.

Laney withdrew three cookies from the plastic sleeve and dunked one in her cold latte. "So? He was cute, you said."

"If he's going to lie about his profession, what else would he hide?"

"You've got a point. Well, good riddance. His loss. There's more fish—"

"Yeah, yeah, yeah. All that. I'm lousy at finding decent men, it's official."

Caro must be depressed for sure, Laney mused, as she watched her friend snitch one of her cookies. *She* was the one who ate when depressed, excited, nervous. Caro turned to cigarettes, or lately to her sugar-free mints.

Laney opened the drawer again and in the back, behind memo pads from the last conference she'd attended, she found some diet butterscotch candies. She silently handed them to Caro.

"Well, that's my story. What about you? From the column this morning, it's obvious you've connected with someone." Caro peeled away the paper from a hard candy and popped it in her mouth.

"I have. With the wrong man." Laney crumbled the last cookie into dust before she swept it onto a scrap piece of paper and tossed it into the trash.

"Grant?"

"Grant."

Caro sat up straight and grinned. "The flirting worked, didn't it? I *knew* it."

"I don't know if it worked or not. But I'm in trouble, Caro. Serious trouble."

"Why? He doesn't feel the same way?"

"Oh, I think he does. You read his column too, right?"

"Yeah. This is great, the whole city following your romance, without even knowing it."

"And they'll follow its failure, too, in a month or so."

"Huh?"

"Grant and I have the column through the end of next month. I have to go out on a couple more dates with new guys, and a couple of follow-up dates, if I can get them. Then, the end." Laney stared at her computer monitor, her eyes tearing slightly at the movement of the abstract figures of the screensaver.

"So, you both move on to other assignments. You'll still be working here, and so will he. You'll be able to see each other without any restraints."

"Not necessarily."

"You mean another co-assignment?"

"No, I mean we may not be here at the paper, maybe not in the same city." Laney glanced at Caro. "This is private info. So if it filters out, you'll be the one I look for."

"You're looking for another job?" Caro whispered, leaning close.

"Not me."

"Oh. Oh, honey. I'm sorry."

"Yeah. Well, like we said, good riddance, more fish, all that." Laney's voice dwindled to nothing and she stared at her friend, no longer trying to hide the tears that welled in her eyes.

Chapter Twelve

She worked through lunch at an almost feverish pace, not tempted by any amount of food. Caro stopped by with a promise to bring back a sandwich but Laney had no heart for a juicy burger or shake.

She called a telephone personals ad and left a message for two men. After hanging up, she jotted down some notes and turned her attention to the last of the obits she had to write up.

Wheaton had finally given the majority of the workload to another junior staff member, and now Laney found herself with time on her hands.

She finished the short synopsis of the eighty-five-year-old veteran's life and sent it out. Sighing, she opened an Internet folder and started to go to the online dating site she'd joined.

Another site in her Favorites file, a few lines down, caught her attention. Jobsearch. *Hmm. What the hey.* She opened the site and a few keystrokes later had a page of positions to review. Now, with the column and the obits experience under her belt, she might have a chance to get a position at another paper.

She sent e-mail queries for four positions and attached a copy of her résumé. Finished, she closed the folder and went to the online dating site. A quick review of the nudges and interest indicators gave her a couple of names and she sent e-mails to those as well then signed off.

Maybe it was better if she left the paper. Working here after Grant left wouldn't be much fun and would evoke too many memories. New sights and new challenges, she figured, couldn't help but refocus her.

She stood and grabbed her purse. Maybe she could catch up with Caro after all.

Grant stood just inside Wheaton's office, waiting for a moment to speak with his superior. Wheaton turned his chair away and proceeded to ignore him so Grant leaned against the door, content to wait. After all, he had a great message to give the jerk. That in a month or so his position at the paper would be vacant. Chew on that, Mr. Editor.

A movement from the back of the room caught his attention and he followed it. Laney walked toward him, her massive purse slung over her shoulder. She wore a light pink blouse tucked into tan slacks and sandals and managed to look attractive, professional, and cool.

He glanced over his shoulder toward the editor then shrugged him off. An hour or so spent with Laney was vastly more interesting than chatting with a man he didn't like or respect anymore. He could talk to Wheaton after lunch.

"Laney! Wait up." He strode to her and smiled. "Lunchtime?"

She kept walking, forcing him to dodge around chairs and desks to keep up.

"Hey, what's the deal? You angry or something?"

"No. Just thinking. Preoccupied, I guess." She exited the newsroom and headed toward the elevator. Grant kept pace with her and punched the down button then angled himself so he could see her profile.

She stood quietly and waited, her natural energy tamped down. What was going on?

"What are you thinking about? Something I can help with?"

"No. Maybe. I don't know yet." The elevator opened and she entered, stepping around a man at the front of the car. Grant followed her and stood close, her perfume enveloping him.

"Like what?" he pressed.

"Maybe later. Oh, I meant to tell you. I've set up a meeting with a couple of guys, one for tomorrow night, the other for the next evening."

"Great." Grant longed for the end of the assignment, when he didn't have to share her time with anyone. "And Craig?"

"I don't think we'll be seeing each other anymore."

"Good, I didn't enjoy trailing you guys all the time." Grant glared at the wide-eyed look he got from the other occupant. "You need something, mister?"

The man grunted and turned away as the elevator opened onto the ground floor. Their elevator mate hesitated, clearly stalling for time. Grant held the open button down and glared the man out of the elevator then ushered Laney out.

She walked by his side into the sunshine. "Let's go to that little sandwich shop we went to the other day."

"I'm not sure I have time—"

"You working on obits today?"

"No, I'm done."

"So, you have time. Let's go, okay? Or do you want something else to eat?"

"No, let's go to the café." She smiled and started toward his car.

"So, what happened with Craig? Not that I care." *Liar.*

"He didn't get what he wanted from me." She waited while he opened her door then sat inside.

Grant hustled around at that and leaned into the opened driver side to glare. "You mean—"

Laney waved a hand in dismissal. "No, no. I handled all that from the first. He wanted free advertising in the paper for his business. When I told him it wouldn't happen, he suddenly lost interest."

"Idiot." Good thing he didn't have to hunt down old Craig.

"No, just someone not interested in me. It's okay." She strapped herself in. He pulled onto the road and headed to the café.

"So, who's the next target, Lois? The guy you met at the car care class?"

"No. I didn't go to the car care class. Found out the only male in the thing was the teacher. Happily married and in his fifties. I did a telephone personals ad instead."

Grant stomped on the brake, narrowly avoiding being rear-ended. "What the—"

"Hold on, Superman. I did my research. This is one that's straight, confidential, and on the up-and-up. Nothing weird or kinky."

"Still, Laney. That seems more dangerous than the other stuff you've been doing."

"You'll be with me, remember? I'm not worried," she softly reassured him.

A nugget of warmth swelled in his chest to the point Grant was sure he couldn't keep it inside. He reached out and squeezed the hand she rested on the top of her shoulder bag in her lap. Laney returned his grasp before letting her hand relax.

"So we do a couple more dates and we're done, huh?"

Now why did he have to bring that up? Ending a relationship that hadn't even had time to develop.

"Yes. I'll try to get a couple of dates out of one of these. Do the second-date thing again. We have to plan our closing columns too." She glanced down at her lap, as if her mind was on something else. But what? She suddenly didn't seem nearly as open as before.

"We have time." He rounded a curve on the country road then pulled into the parking lot of the café.

"Right, time." She opened her door before he could get to her and strode to the café.

They got a table immediately and placed their orders. "What's going on, Laney? You're hiding something."

She looked at him for a long minute before answering. "I sent out a few feelers for jobs this morning. I guess I'm preoccupied about them."

The warm glow inside Grant congealed into a cold block. She might leave? "Jobs in town?"

"No. All over. San Francisco, New York, Philadelphia. And Tampa. That one looks the most promising, I think."

"You're leaving the paper?"

"If I can find something else." She smiled ruefully. "The column may help with that."

"Yeah. You've done a good job with it."

"You want ketchup?" The waitress set a couple of burger plates in front of them and held a ketchup bottle aloft. Grant nodded absently, more to get her to leave than anything.

"Great. Burgers. Let's eat." Laney smothered her fries in ketchup and started. Grant's appetite disappeared.

That night Grant pulled a beer out of his refrigerator and opened it. He roamed through the kitchen and into the living room, located his remote and flipped on the television. A game was on, the perfect way to relax after a long day of work.

After a few minutes, he began to surf through the cable channels absently before realization hit. He was turning the Braves off. The man who stayed up for four days straight to win a pair of tickets to the playoffs in college, who used money he had saved for a car to buy season tickets his first year in Atlanta, had turned off a game.

Disgusted, Grant chugged the last of his beer and crushed the can. He leaned his elbows on his knees, dropped his head and groaned. What was the deal? The column, while not a preferred assignment, was going well, and garnering both him and Laney good reviews. His prospects for a new job had never been better. And Laney . . . Laney was the best thing he'd run across in years.

That was it. Laney and Chicago. The two didn't mesh, especially since she had started looking for a job of her own. In another town. His groan turned into a growl. How could he hope to continue a relationship with her when they might be on opposite sides of the country?

"God. A relationship." He was officially over the deep end. He threw the remote onto the couch and stood. He had to get out of here. Now.

He paced around the room, going through the options

for the evening in his mind. A bar? No, he didn't want to make a bad evening worse by drowning in self-pity. He could call some friends and play a game of pickup basketball, except he didn't want to answer questions that inevitably would come up about his absence lately.

No, what he really wanted to do was spend some time with Laney. He put aside his pride and grabbed the phone to call her.

Laney hustled around her living room and rushed to put things to order. Grant's call, while a surprise, was welcome, but worrying. Did he want to deepen their relationship? She couldn't deal with more serious contact, not with him leaving in a month. Or worse, did he want to end the embryonic thing they called a relationship? She couldn't bear thinking of either option, let alone anything in between.

"Probably wants to give me grief over something I did with the column." She plumped an already fat pillow and returned it on the sofa. After another circuit through the living room and kitchen of the suddenly too small apartment, she plopped onto the sofa to wait.

Grant arrived within twenty minutes with a rented movie and snacks. She popped the popcorn in the microwave and set them up with sodas while he fiddled with the VCR.

"Why don't you have a DVD player?" He came to the sofa and sat beside her, handing her the remote.

"I didn't want to replace all of my tapes."

"Honey, you'll have to one day soon, so you might as well face the inevitable." He draped an arm across her shoulders and leaned back to watch the film, an action adventure with plenty of special effects.

"Not until I have to."

A few minutes passed and she tried to concentrate on the movie, but had more luck reveling in the warmth of his palm through the shirt covering her shoulder.

"Laney, about your job searches—"

"I haven't heard anything, yet." She clenched a handful of popcorn tensely, before dropping it back into the bowl in her lap.

"Have you checked in Chicago?"

"Chicago?" She glanced at him, surprised to see a slight flush run across his cheeks.

"Yeah. I thought if you found a job in the city, we could still see each other, you know?"

Laney turned her gaze to the television; Grant didn't need to get a look at her expression. Of course, he'd only see confusion.

She stared blankly at the images of a buff couple, both perfectly coifed in the middle of a jungle battle. Her expectations for the evening, vague though they were, hadn't even approached this.

"Laney? What do you think? Willing to try it?" His hand pressed into her shoulder with a light but persistent pressure.

"Why?"

"We'd be able to keep seeing each other, continue our relationship."

She shook her head, partly to clear the fog his comments engendered as well as to give her opinion. "Grant, I'm not sure we *have* a relationship."

She interrupted his response with a raised hand. "No, let me finish. I'm not saying we don't enjoy each other's company and want to see each other, but we haven't gone far enough to build a relationship or to make that kind of commitment."

"How far do we have to go? I wanted to take it slow, not rush things." Laney felt acutely the cool air as he removed his arm from around her and leaned forward to retrieve his soda.

"I agree. But, don't you think me moving to Chicago is going too fast?"

Grant frowned at the melting ice in his glass. "I guess so."

She laid her hand on his forearm, pulling his gaze to her. "I want to see you more, I really do. But I can't see me moving to a city just because we happen to like dating each other. And we've not really dated outside the context of the column. What would happen if we found out that we really didn't have anything in common outside of this assignment?"

"Enough, already. I give up." He slumped into the cushions.

Laney leaned into his shoulder and smiled when he took the hint to wrap his arm around her again. She offered him the popcorn with one last piece of advice. "We're accepting the inevitable, right?"

"Right," he agreed, but didn't look too happy.

Chapter Thirteen

"Let's sit over there." Fred, her latest date, gestured toward a shadowed corner table in the coffee shop. Laney gritted her teeth into a semblance of a smile, and let him lead her to the table.

The last week had passed with little movement on the dating front. Her online personals dwindled to a trickle and the newspaper ad revealed more attached men than eligible. Something she found totally disgusting. Then, two days ago, she got a response from her telephone personals ad. Fred, thirty-two, single, and looking for companionship. What could be better? Better could be that she sat with Grant, not another guy.

Once seated, she requested iced tea and waited while

Fred filled their orders. When he returned, he carried a slice of cheesecake. With two forks. On a first date. *Yew.*

"Dig in, sugar." He handed her a fork and leered. She accepted the utensil but lacked an appetite for dessert.

"Maybe later. Listen, tell me about yourself. What kind of law do you practice?" She set the fork aside discreetly.

"Divorce. I'm the third-best divorce lawyer in town." He dug into the cheesecake with relish. "I've gotten higher settlements than anyone else in my firm this year."

"Great." Did he notice her sarcasm? Probably not.

"Yeah. I pride myself in getting the most for my client. No matter what it takes."

And that was attractive to someone, she was sure. But not her. Laney suppressed a sigh and furtively glanced at her watch. Seven-fifteen. Lord. Only fifteen minutes down, how long to go before the date ended? She couldn't in good conscience end the date before eight o'clock. Could she?

A glance around the shop revealed Grant, four tables away, partially hidden behind a novel, a grin on his face. He thought this was funny! Well, she thought, he'd get his some day.

The conversation lingered on; Fred and his job, Fred and his hobbies of collecting old law records and matchbooks, Fred and his bulldog. Apparently, Fred's favorite subject of discourse was Fred.

The end of the date, thank God, came with the last of

the cheesecake and coffees. Laney excused herself to the restroom and then made her escape. "Fred, I've had a lovely time, but I have to work tomorrow morning."

"You said you write for *The Globe*?" He stood and hitched up his pants.

"Uh huh." She'd mentioned her job at the beginning of the evening. Surprisingly, he hadn't forgotten while bragging about his wins and custody battles.

She edged toward the door. He cut her off at the corner of the table and Laney shifted her purse from her shoulder to her front to form a barrier between them.

"I bet you get a lot of good tips at your job." He stepped closer to her and Laney glimpsed movement out of the corner of her eye.

"Not really. My last long assignment was writing obituaries for the paper." *Now move so I can go home and shower this feeling away.*

"Yeah. Tough job. But I bet you get some great stories on the city beat. You know where all the bodies are buried." He stepped closer, touching her shoulder bag in the process. *Gross. Now, I'll have to have it cleaned.*

"Listen, sweetheart. Let's get together again. I know this club on the south side. The KitKat Club. Heard of it?"

"Yeah. Not really what I like to do in my spare time, though." She didn't relish the idea of watching topless waitresses being groped by letches like Fred.

"You'll like it. I know it. And we could get to know each other better. A lot better." He moved in for the kill, or the wallop of her purse. His hand extended toward her, right below her shoulder, much too close for comfort.

She pulled her arm back, taking her purse with her, in a wind-up her father had taught her. Before she could deliver the pitch, though, Fred suddenly retreated several feet. But not on his own.

Grant's hand left Fred's collar as soon as he was out of touching distance. Laney glared at both men, unsure of which one she was most angry at.

Fred's face was beet-red. "I'll sue—"

"No you won't. Not at the risk of being found out," Grant growled.

"Found out?"

"That you, a renowned divorce attorney, was seen manhandling an innocent woman in a public place." Grant stepped forward, his glare fierce.

"Grant! I can handle this," Laney said only to be ignored by both men.

"I wasn't touching her," Fred protested but retreated. He scurried out of the coffee shop without a backward glance.

Laney scowled at Grant. "What do you think you were doing?"

"I was saving your pretty little hide."

"You thought I couldn't handle it myself?" Her voice rose and she tried to control her anger.

"Not by the way you acted, no." He advanced, towering over her.

Laney planted her fists on her hips, her purse hanging from a wrist, weighing her down. "And you think I can't manage a few jerks when you're not around?"

"No."

"And when you're in Chicago, freezing your . . . nose off, I won't be able to fend off men?" She stepped up, her face within inches of his shirt collar.

"That's right." Grant leaned down until said nose almost touched hers.

Laney retreated one step and yanked her arm back, catching the bag in her hand. The oversized purse arced and slammed into Grant's stomach. "Well, you'll never know, will you? 'Cause when you're in Chicago, I'll be here in Atlanta, dating someone else."

"Damn, what's in that thing? Bricks?" he wheezed, his hand clutching his stomach.

"Yeah. Just the thing for a poor defenseless woman in the city." She stomped out of the café, ignoring the giggles, the murmurs, the doubled-over figure of the man she loved.

Grant thanked the waitress and folded the plastic bag of ice in a napkin then gingerly laid it against his abdomen, wincing as he did so. He'd been kidding about the bricks, but it felt like bricks and a couple of rocks too.

He remained at her abandoned table, trying to get his breath back. He'd probably made a huge mistake, butting in like that. But when the jerk advanced on her the way he did, all Grant could think of was getting her out of danger. Out of the way of someone who could hurt her.

Apparently, he'd done what her date couldn't, hurt her feelings.

He grimaced as he stretched to retrieve his cell phone from his pants pocket. He dialed her number— she'd had time to get home. If not, he'd call her cell.

Cold water seeped out of the bag and onto his shirt, prompting him to grab more napkins and layer them between him and the makeshift ice pack.

She picked up on the third ring. "Hello?"

"Hey, it's me."

She didn't respond, but didn't hang up either, which was a good sign. Maybe.

"Can I come over?"

"Why?" She sounded sullen. Grant wanted to see that, see her mouth pulled into a pout.

"So I can apologize in person."

"I can hear you fine on the phone."

"But you can't see the contrite look in my eyes when I tell you how much of a jerk I am."

A pause gave him hope she would relent, then she came back with: "Practice on the phone."

He hid a chuckle. If she heard him laugh now, he was in the doghouse for sure. "I am sorry, Lois. I know you can take care of yourself. I just get a little nuts when I see a guy coming on to you."

"Why should you?"

"You know why."

Another pause.

"Can I come over?" He could eat crow with the best of them, if he had to.

Several more seconds passed. "Okay."

He raced from the coffee shop, his stomach suddenly less achy than before. As he drove he planned his speech; what to say, to promise her.

She opened the door to Grant's knock. Just outside he stood with a peace offering.

"Where did you get those?" Laney said, eyeing the beautiful arrangement.

"I was driving down the street and saw them in the shop window and thought of you. Like them?" He offered them to her with a smile as he entered.

Laney held the overflowing basket reverently and sighed. "This is so thoughtful of you, thanks."

She smiled at him and Grant's grin broadened and he reached toward a pink bloom in the basket. "That one looks pretty good."

Laney plucked the flower from the container and took a large bite from it. "You know me too well."

"Well, I just figured you'd appreciate a basket of cookies shaped like flowers more than the real thing."

"You figured right. Sit down, want something to drink?" She carried the basket to the bar and set it in the center of the counter before heading to the cabinet and coffeemaker.

"Maybe in a few minutes. First, I wanted to talk to you."

"Grant, you don't have to—"

He came into the kitchen and grasped her by the upper arms. "I do. I'm sorry I didn't give you enough credit tonight. I saw that jerk close in on you and I didn't think twice. I just reacted."

"And so did I." She stood in his hold, content, yet wanting to be closer.

"Yeah, well . . . I guess I'm just not used to standing around watching another man move in on my girl."

"Your girl?" She grinned and arched her eyebrow at the same time. "Are we in junior high?"

"I felt like it tonight." He shrugged and caressed her cheek with a gentle hand. "I wanted to deck that guy and he hadn't even touched you."

"And he wouldn't have. But thanks for believing that I could have handled it."

He pulled her into a tight hug and held her for a moment before releasing her. Clearing his throat he rounded the bar and removed a cookie from the basket. He munched on the chocolate-flavored rose. "You said something about a drink?"

She turned and filled the carafe of the coffeemaker and quickly set up the brew cycle. In a few minutes, the smell of hazelnut filled the room and she poured two cups. As she handed him his coffee, he arched a brow.

"Live a little," she encouraged, and he sipped it cautiously. Apparently it passed muster since he took a longer swallow of the brew before biting into his cookie again.

They made short work of the cookies until all that was left at the bottom of the basket was some plastic filler and a folded sheet of paper. Laney picked it up and unfolded it. In untidy scribble, the note was short but very sweet to read.

You're cordially invited to accompany an apologetic Grant on a classic movie date, complete with popcorn, mints, and a gallon of soda. Handholding optional.

"When are we going?" Her voice quivered with excitement.

He grinned and pressed a light kiss on her lips. "Go get dressed, I'll check and see what's playing tonight."

"I thought you said this was a classic movie," she whispered as she delved into the popcorn vat Grant held.

"It's a classic movie date, Lois. Not a classic movie. Don't you like it?" Grant draped an arm over the back of her seat, his hand grazing her shoulder.

"I love it and Sandra Bullock's my favorite actress. I'm just surprised, that's all. Mints?" She offered him the long box of chocolate candy. Grant shook his head and settled into his seat.

The movie, a romantic comedy, held his attention for

the entire evening. Or maybe it was Laney's smile, and her laughter at the star's antics on screen. Or her tendency to lean toward him as if she wanted to share the joy of watching the film.

Halfway through the movie, he pulled his arm away from her shoulder and tucked her hand in his. For over thirty minutes he was content with comparing the dainty fingers he held with his own larger ones, the softness of her skin against his rougher palm.

By the end of the film, he leaned over and whispered in her ear, "Ready for the most classic moment of the movie?"

She looked at him, her face turned up toward his. "What's that?"

"The romantic kiss," he murmured and leaned in. Her kiss, flavored with butter, salt and mint, mesmerized him.

He pulled away as the closing credits scrolled up the screen and the lights rose in the theater. He stood and held his hand out for her.

"We missed the end of the movie."

She tucked her hand in his and walked close at his side. "I liked your ending better anyway."

They spent the drive home in conversation about the movie, the column, and trying more flavored flowers. All the way, Laney's hand rested in his. At her door, he cupped her cheek in his hand and kissed her. When Laney leaned forward he wrapped his arms around her, pulling her into a tight embrace.

"Want more coffee?" she whispered.

"Um um. Can't. Got to go." Every word he murmured against her lips, every syllable a caress.

"'Kay."

"See you in the morning." He lowered his arms and stepped away, the warmth of his body leaving hers. But his mouth remained on hers.

"Good night." She drew back reluctantly.

Grant stared over Laney's cubicle partition. "Hey, honey."

Her smile bright, she glanced up from her computer. A light blush crept across her cheeks and he ached to kiss the soft skin, see if the flush increased the warmth of her flesh.

"Hi."

"Are you busy?"

"Just getting some notes down about the telephone personals ad and date. I didn't have a lot of time to do that last night," she teased.

"I hadn't thought of the column. Guess I need to do some writing on it too."

"We could go over it together. Want to come over for dinner tonight? We can review the ideas I have for the last installment." She leaned back in her chair with a creak and wobble.

"I can't. I got a call before I left the house this morning. From my contact in Chicago."

"Oh."

"I've got to fly out for another interview."

"When?" Her expression remained calm, no unease reflected at all.

Grant stepped into her space and leaned over to pluck a writer Snoopy figurine from the computer monitor. "Tonight. I'm taking the red-eye this evening, be back tomorrow. Can we talk then?"

"Sure. I'll jot down some notes and we can go over them day after tomorrow."

So the invitation for dinner didn't last past another trip to Chicago.

"Want to get some lunch later?"

"I don't think so, I want to get ahead on the column."

"Right. Well, I'll be back soon and we'll talk." He wanted more from her than an occasional date and a brush off. And he was determined to get it—if he could figure out a way to handle the new job offer and her in Atlanta.

The flight, crowded and noisy, didn't lend much in the way of thought and contemplation. By the time he arrived at the hotel Grant was exhausted and frustrated by Laney's apathy. If she'd been mad it would have shown she felt something. He *knew* she felt something. The kiss after the movies proved she was attracted to him. And if she found him attractive, she had to have some feelings for him. He just had to decide if he wanted the job more, or her.

The next morning, after a sleepless night, he met the

managing editor of the newspaper. He sat through a glowing report of his abilities, expectations of the paper in his position of city beat reporter, and then put off acceptance for a week. Then, instead of staying the evening and meeting his old college roommate for a drink and looking for a new home as he'd planned last month, he found a seat on the next plane home.

By seven in the evening, he was at Laney's front door, waiting for her to answer his knock.

Her outfit, a pair of uneven cut-off jeans and a ratty T-shirt, only set off her innate beauty. Grant accepted her offer of a cup of coffee and sat in an armchair.

"Well? Did they offer you the job?" She perched on the edge of the sofa then popped up. "What am I saying? Of course they offered you the job, you're the best. They'll be lucky to have you. When are you—"

"Laney, take a breath. I haven't accepted it yet."

"You haven't?" Again she sat, this time lowering herself into the seat slowly as if afraid to shatter a mood. She picked up her cup and hid her face in it.

"I asked them to give me a week to decide."

"Why?"

Grant placed his coffee cup on the end table and tried to catch her eye. He needed her to understand him, this time.

"I needed to think about it, Laney. Talk to you about it."

"What's to talk about? Grant this is a great opportunity. You'd get to cover important news stories, make a difference, just like you've always wanted, but not had the opportunity to do here."

She rose and collected their cups. On her way to the kitchen, she threw over her shoulder, "I think you need to take it."

"And you? The column?"

She rinsed their cups in the sink, her back to him. "Me? I'll keep looking for another job."

"So the leads you had in Florida and the other cities didn't pan out?" He tried to keep the relief out of his voice.

"Nope, but there are more jobs out there, and I'll keep writing and trying to get more bylines. As for the column, it's almost over, anyway. A relief for both of us, don't you think?"

"Right. And what about the fact that we've been dating?"

"Dating isn't commitment, Grant, remember?" she dismissed with a bright smile. The smile resembled those she presented to her column dates—false, a mask.

"Commitment?"

"Yeah, remember the thing you don't believe in? Marriage, kids, the whole nine yards." She shrugged. "That's all I'll settle for, and it's not something we can achieve over a long-distance relationship. Or in a liaison established by assignment."

"So all this was the column."

"Sure. What else would it have been?"

Without a word he turned and stalked from the apartment, leaving her with her plans and commitment.

Laney closed the door behind her with a groan. She had held it together while Grant was there, but now she wanted to dive into a pint of ice cream, or maybe a quart. She headed to the kitchen, only to be waylaid by the phone's ring.

"Hello?"

"How was it?"

"Hey, Caro. It went fine."

"Fine? So Grant didn't get the offer?"

Laney tucked the portable phone between her shoulder and chin and entered the kitchen. She opened the cabinet and pulled out a bowl and spoon. "No. He got the offer."

"And did you talk about you two?"

"Kind of. We talked about the fact we don't have a relationship. He's going to Chicago, remember?" Her stomach growled and she scrounged in the refrigerator freezer for a full pint.

"So you didn't even try? You just gave up?" Caro sounded exasperated.

"What's the use? Put me and dating, writing a column that he hates, and working for an editor who sees Grant as a threat, against a city desk job in Chicago. Which one would you choose if you were Grant?"

"I'd choose the person I loved. Don't you realize how lucky you are? You've found the one person who makes you complete, who cares for you despite the fact that you drive him crazy, that you can drive everyone crazy. We're all looking for that, you know? And it fell into your lap. Fight for it!"

Laney stared into the depths of the Ben and Jerry's container, totally out of the mood to eat. But definitely in the mood to cry for a few days.

Chapter Fourteen

"Morgan, I need to see you and Stone in fifteen minutes." Wheaton's voice sounded tinny in the telephone receiver. Laney cut the connection and returned to her work.

She'd spent the morning trying to get Grant's visit last night out of her mind. Instead, she worked on a new proposal, an exposé on personals ads and their pitfalls. It looked promising. With her experience with The Single Life column and contacts she'd made, maybe she could win over the editor and get another byline. And maybe pigs would sprout wings and flutter around their heads.

She dreaded meeting Wheaton. Having to face the fact that Grant would be leaving in a short time. What should she do in the interim, before he left Atlanta?

Should she spend every moment she had with him or cut off the budding relationship now, when the chances of being hurt were minimal?

Who was she kidding? Even if she stopped seeing him now, the pain would sever her heart.

Grant's cubicle remained empty. In fact it looked as if he hadn't been in that morning. What was going on? Had he decided to go back to Chicago after their talk last night? Was he on another assignment for the paper?

She ran to the bathroom, her eyes filling. God, she couldn't cry in front of him. On the way, she tapped Caroline's desk with a frantic hand and motioned for her friend to follow.

Once inside, she turned the water on. The splash into the basin hid her sobs as she buried her face in her hands. After a few minutes, she became aware of Caro's hand on her shoulder and accepted the tissue extended to her.

"Why'd I let him go to that last interview without telling him? I'm an idiot."

"You're human, afraid of getting hurt, just like the rest of us."

Laney splashed her face with water before turning it off. "I was still too much of a coward to tell him I love him," she sniffed.

"And it's too late?" Caro strolled to the paper towel machine and wedged her hand behind it.

"Yes. He's not even in the office. He's getting ready to leave, Caro. Otherwise, he would be working on something. Anything. The only times he's out of the newsroom are when he's working on an assignment or when he's with me, and I know he's not working on another story and . . . what are you doing?" She observed as her friend twisted her hand to push it farther into the narrow space between the wall and towel machine.

Caroline pulled a crushed pack of cigarettes out from the small space behind the dispenser. She pried it open and removed a flattened cigarette. "What does it look like? I'm jumping off the wagon."

Laney yanked the pack from her hand, turned to the basin and held it under the flowing water. After she doused the whole package she dropped the soggy mess in the trash.

She rounded on her friend. "You were tossing away every effort you made at quitting that nasty habit for a stale, smelly break? After you tried so hard?"

Caro advanced on Laney, her finger pointing in accusation. "And what about you? Huh? Did you listen to me last night? Did you even think about what I said? He's perfect for you, Laney. And if you don't take a chance on him and your relationship, you're never going to get out of that dating rut."

Laney checked her watch in resignation. "Well, just because I'm a failure doesn't mean you need to be one too. It's time for my meeting with Wheaton." She glanced quickly at her reflection in the mirror before leaving the room. A hand through her hair made it look a bit better but there was little she could do for her reddened eyes.

The way to the editor's office stretched out before her, the last mile. She'd advanced a few steps when Grant waylaid her, taking her arm, and pulling her through the room, out the door and into the hall. In the distance a lone passenger entered the elevator, leaving them alone.

"I need to talk to you." He braced an arm against the wall she leaned against, enclosing her in his warmth. She was going to miss that.

"No kidding. We're late for our meeting with Wheaton. What's up?" She scanned his face. She had to remember it, the sharp planes, the five o'clock shadow. Oh Lord, how maudlin could she get?

"The end of the column. Chicago. Us."

"We're at the end of the column, and—"

Jim Cole stuck his head through the hallway door. "You guys, Wheaton's on the warpath. You better get in there now, if you want to keep your jobs."

Grant grimaced and shot a look toward Cole. "Give us a couple of minutes."

Laney lost whatever nerve she'd gained in the bathroom and dodged around Grant. She scurried into the newsroom and back toward her cubicle.

Grant shifted restlessly in his chair, his eye on the door of Wheaton's office. Where was she?

He'd run late that morning and hadn't had time to

talk to her before their meeting with the editor, what with her escape act from the hall. Now, it looked as if he would have to dump the news on her at the same time Wheaton heard it.

"I'm giving her five minutes," Wheaton warned.

"And after that?"

Wheaton glared at him and Grant didn't bother to suppress his grin.

"Let's get to this, Stone."

"Not until Laney gets here."

"Laney's here. What's up?" She entered the room, closed the door, and slid into the interview chair beside him, facing Wheaton.

"We were about to talk about the future of the column. While it's been accepted by the majority of the readership, several of the editors have found the column to be a flash in the pan. I wanted to give you the opportunity to leave the endeavor—"

"I thought the column ended with this last edition?" She glanced around the room as if the desk itself would clear up the matter.

Before anyone could answer her, the door of the office opened and an older, distinguished but rumpled man entered. Unlike Wheaton, who resembled a CEO, James Phipps looked the part of a harried newspaper man.

Wheaton shot out of his seat and into almost a military attention.

"Ms. Morgan, gentlemen. Let's get to business, shall we?" James Phipps, managing editor of *The Globe*, commandeered the seat behind Wheaton's desk, which left the city beat editor to find another seat. He pulled a straight-backed wooden chair out of the newsroom and perched on it stiffly.

A great strategic move on Phipps' part. Grant stifled another grin and blatantly settled into his cushioned armchair, his gaze on the managing editor.

"Stone, Morgan, The Single Life column has been a resounding success. So much of a success that we've decided to extend it indefinitely."

Laney's expression brightened then abruptly shifted as she met Grant's gaze. He smiled slightly at her. *Jeez, I wish I'd had time to explain before springing this on her.*

Laney cleared her throat. "Sir. I was under the impression that The Single Life ended with this week's column."

"The original version, yes. We have plans to revamp it, somewhat."

"But what if we have other plans?" Laney pressed.

Grant, seeing she planned to support him no matter what, interrupted.

"Mr. Phipps, would you mind explaining about the expansion?"

Phipps smiled expansively. "We want to expand the column to encompass more. More couples, more cities. When Ms. Morgan goes out on dates—"

"That's something we need to negotiate," Grant interrupted.

"Really?" Phipps' eyebrow rose.

"What?"

He ignored both the managing editor's and Laney's questions.

"And the rest of the development?" Grant urged Phipps to continue.

"Assuming the column does as well over the next six months that it has done in its first segment, we syndicate it to the other Gaines Group newspapers. That means you and Ms. Morgan would oversee a syndicate of thirteen cities, thirteen newspapers.

"Also, if you're interested, you could do some corollary articles on the pitfalls of the singles scene in the various cities."

Laney's inhalation drew Grant's gaze. Excitement, combined with apprehension filled her eyes. Grant stood, holding a hand out to her as he addressed Phipps.

"We need a couple of minutes, sir. If you'll excuse us."

Laney rose and, placing her hand in his, accompanied him from the room. Once in the hallway again, Grant leaned his back against the wall, facing her.

"Well, sweetheart? What do you think? Want to do this for another six months, maybe more?"

"I'm not sure. Phipps isn't counting on one of us leaving. I guess I could try to talk him into—"

"I'm not going anywhere." He straightened and stepped toward her.

She looked at him in consternation. "But you went to Chicago, interviewed."

"And I called the newspaper this morning. I declined their offer, honey."

"But why? That's all you ever wanted."

Grant took the remaining step necessary to bring her into touching range. He brushed a curl away from her forehead before cupping her cheek. "I have all I ever wanted right here, with you."

"You do?" she whispered.

"Yep. I love you. Smart mouth and all." He leaned forward and kissed her.

Laney leaned into his embrace with a sigh. Grant gave into the temptation and lengthened the kiss, ignoring two editors waiting for them. After a few moments he broke off the kiss and gently pushed Laney away.

"Well? Aren't you going to tell me you love me?" he demanded.

"I didn't have a chance, you were kissing me."

"Well, I'm not going to again, unless you tell me."

Laney giggled at the disgruntled sound in his voice and complied, after which he gave her a very satisfactory kiss. Finally, with reluctance he drew away.

"Honey, we need to decide. Do you want to go on with the column? Or do we go turn it down, ask for something else?"

"What about your need to do something else more newsworthy? Hard-hitting journalism?"

His fingers smoothed her cheek again. "The column will allow that. Corollary articles on the underground single scenes can be hard-hitting as they come, even to the extent of getting national coverage, especially with syndication."

After a moment's silence she smiled. "We continue. We took a lousy idea and made it into something special."

He grinned then sobered quickly. "But I don't want you to date every guy coming down the pike."

"I wouldn't have to." She headed back to the news-room and the editor's office. She threw back over her shoulder, "I think I have the perfect volunteer for the guinea pig position."

That afternoon, after a very satisfying lunch and planning session, Laney sat and wrote the last article for The Single Life column.

Isn't it surprising what can happen when you open yourself up to love? You find that your neighbor, workmate, friend next door is the love you've been looking for. For me, the one I was looking for was the person by my side all along. And this column helped me to find him. All the more reason to cel-ebrate the continuation of The Single Life. But what surprises we have in store for you, and maybe even for our next single lady. While I won't continue to date and check out the singles scene firsthand, I'll be along for the ride.

Grant chuckled as he wrote the last installment. Who knew when he started, how it would turn out?

If you haven't guessed yet, I'll be the one who announces the semiretirement of our single lady. If I have anything to say about it, she won't be single too much longer. But don't fret, Laney's still going to be around, she'll join me as a silent observer. And the resident dater, Caro, will share her experiences in the single world. So read on, there's more to share in the world of The Single Life.